The Zarder

Sara Jo Easton

© Sara Melissa Miller 2011

First Edition

ISBN 978-0-615-51706-3

Printed by 48HrBooks (48HrBooks.com)

All rights reserved. No part of this book may be reproduced in any form or by any electronic or mechanical means without permission in writing by the author, except by a reviewer, who may quote brief passages in a review.

This is a work of fiction. Names, characters, businesses, organizations and places and events are either from the author's imagination or used fictitiously. Any resemblance to actual persons, living or dead, events or locations is completely coincidental and, in the author's opinion, incredibly bizarre.

To my family and friends, who have been wonderfully supportive on this journey I have taken, and to all of the teachers in my life, especially Mr. Tinlin, who taught me how to read.

Prologue, Or A Tale the Onizards Tell Their Children Under the Starlight

At the beginning of time, the Great Lord of the Sky created the world. Upon his command, the barren rock turned to precious fields of oats, vast forests, mighty seas, and the tall, proud mountains. Then, when the world was finished, the Lord realized that there was something missing in the world. For, though he was mightier than the seas and taller than the tallest of mountains, he was lonely. Without any living creatures, the world itself was a waste of effort. Thus, when all was prepared, he created the Onizards, humans, and other creatures of the world.

The Great Lord of the Sky loved variety, and so he made certain that the world was populated with many good elements. From the deepest part of the mountains, he created the Children of Fire, Onizards with the power to breathe flame. From the soil he created the Children of Earth, Onizards with incredible powers of healing. From the strongest gusts of the first storm he created the small but swift Children of Wind, and from the rain itself he created the Children of Water.

All seemed right in the world at first, but there was no light. The Lord had saved this for the right time, but without the light the Onizards could not see they were all the same race with different abilities. Demons amongst the various Children persuaded them to be heartless and cruel toward the other elements, and many unspeakable crimes occurred during that time that would cause the majority of modern Onizards to hang their heads in shame. In one terrible battle, the Children of Fire destroyed the homes and nesting grounds of the Children of Water. When hope for the Water Children seemed lost, and the last daughter of the Water Chieftain was about to be incinerated along with the rest of her clan, Senbralfi, son of the Fire Chieftain, threw himself between the two clans and sacrificed himself to save her life.

The Child of Fire had been the first being in the world to truly love another, and this did not go unnoticed by the Great Lord of the Sky. Instead of letting the young Onizard die, the Lord bestowed in him the light so desperately needed in the world, and he became Senbralni, the first Child of Light.

While Senbralni lived, all saw that he was a blessed Onizard, and they became united under his command. He guided them in building a new home where the homes of the Water Children once stood, and they built a new nesting location high above the ground. They called the new home the Sandleyr, and they called Senbralni the Leyrkan, heart of their home. The few who did not accept him were driven out of the united Onizard clan to be killed by the human tribes.

When all of his work was finished, Senbralni relinquished his physical form to become part of the sky itself. Though this new sun was a powerful source of light for half of the time of the world, it was not all of the light that had been given to Senbralni. The remaining light divided among all of the creatures of the world, though it did not divide equally. Most of it went to Senbralni's four children, who became the new Children of Light.

It was then that they discovered their father's secret, both a blessing and a curse; with the powers of Light came the power to feel the emotions and pain of all around them. Together they decided to divide their ruling duties, for none of them could handle their new powers on their own. Telgrasan and Marulsan ruled during the time their father was in the sky; Maraeni and Mebralni ruled when their father was not in the sky. This system of a Day Kingdom and a Night Kingdom worked well throughout the years to maintain order and stability in the Sandleyr. When one Child of Light died, his or her chosen heir would gain the powers of Light. The chain continued unbroken until Ammasan of the Day Kingdom died without naming her heir.

In the resulting chaos, Deybralfi, daughter of Ammasan, claimed the title of Queen and turned the Sandleyr toward a dark path. Human beings were captured and forced into slave labor for the self-proclaimed Fire Queen, and Onizards neglected to give respect to the remaining Children of Light, even going out of their way to avoid the Leyrkan of the Night Kingdom. Some would say that they even forgot how to love, for during that time there were no mothers tenderly guarding their eggs.

Throughout this, the saying of Senmani, a former ruler of the Night Kingdom, entered the hearts of those still loyal to the path of good Onizards: love will keep you strong, even when all strengths fail. Perhaps that can explain the strange tale of the Zarder.

Chapter 1

Those with eyes on the clouds knew that a storm would be coming. The wind was moving faster than normal, and the trees in the distance were swaying under the pressure. Even the normally calm sea was crashing against the sandstone wall that seemed meant to keep everyone from the water as much as it protected the beach from the elements. The wall wrapped around a towering structure that stretched into a bowl shape at the top. The structure was built with the same sandstone as the wall, and some crumbling pieces of stone at the top were clues that it had weathered many storms in the past.

For most of the inhabitants of the Sandleyr, as this strange place was called, the storm was of no importance; it was just a simple inconvenience for anyone wishing to go outside. The majority of them were relaxing underground, in the large rock cavern beneath the sandy beach. There were still some on the surface, however, whose views on the storm varied from joy to trepidation.

Near the entrance to the underground portions of the Sandleyr was a dragon-like creature that made the giant boulder he was standing on look like a mere rock. His large ears seemed to hold two horns in place as they curved around the top of his head. Another horn protruded from a small tuft of white hair on his forehead, making his head seem larger than it actually was. His body was thin to the point of being almost deformed, and his tail, formed into a fin at the end, was long and lanky. But his eyes, which were like firm islands of lavender in the cerulean sea that formed his face and body, held a gaze that made up for his lacking physical attributes. Those proud but suffering eyes were fixed intently on the storm clouds as if to hide his feelings from the second creature standing nearby.

She seemed smaller than the blue creature at first glance, but this was because she held her wings against her side instead of in the air as he did. She was of the same species as he was, though her skin was pale green in hue and her tail tapered into a leaf-like shape at the end. She held a smile on her face as she viewed the clouds, though her light green eyes betrayed it as a forced one.

We need the rain. It will be a refreshing change after the drought we've been having, the green creature said through the telepathic communication of their species.

Maybe you need the rain, but I do not, the blue creature responded, blasting a large dent into the sand with a jet stream of water from his mouth. *As much as I used to enjoy rainy days, Rulsaesan's eggs may be affected by this weather, and I do not want to see them harmed.*

I'm certain Rulsaesan and Deyraeno will take care of their eggs, Idenno, the green creature said softly, as if in fear of being attacked. *They won't let their children be harmed when they have waited so long for them. At worst, the poor Onizard children will turn out to be Children of Water like you.*

The Onizard called Idenno smirked. *That's fine, as long as they don't end up being Children of Earth like the mighty Teltrena.*

Don't be improper, Teltrena said, suddenly showing even greater discomfort. *I am not legally a Child of Earth. Besides, why did you say you used to enjoy rainy days? I still see you dancing with glee whenever even a tiny rainfall comes to the Sandleyr.*

Idenno's smirk faded. *While it is true that I still dance, it is not from joy. When I feel the steady rhythm of the raindrops on my wings, I cannot help but dance. Water is my element, after all. But when I dance, whenever I pause at just the right moment...*he said before turning his head away from Teltrena, leaving the rest unsaid.

At this, the green Onizard turned noticeably paler. *I am sorry if I upset you, honorable Idenno.*

Honorable? the Child of Water made an attempt at laughter before frowning. *Being forced to work for the Fire Queen brings me no honor. Even if it did, I would forsake the title of Watchzard if I didn't have a promise to keep and things worth protecting. Being honorable is useless when you have no happiness.*

Teltrena's mental voice shook as she said, *At least you have respect left. Not even my mother considers me a worthy Onizard, and I'll probably never be allowed to use my healing*

7

powers again. I am a non-nature, the scourge of the Sandleyr; my very existence is useless. Even being the Fire Queen's messenger is a step above what I should be allowed to do.

Don't say things like that, scolded Idenno. *You are a Child of Earth in the hearts of those that matter, and you are a very useful Onizard. If I had any respect left, I'd let you have all of it. But I don't, and it's not worth us both getting upset from debating over this. Don't you need to report to the Fire Queen? I don't want her suspecting a nonexistent conspiracy.*

Yes, of course, the non-nature said. *I'd better get down there now. But will you be able to continue standing up here like this?*

I have no choice. The Watchzard said with a sigh. *I'll just hold on to my desperate hope that things will get better.*

It is all that any of us can do, Teltrena said, spreading her wings and flying underground.

After he watched her leave, Idenno turned back to watching the approaching storm, a calmly dismal expression on his face the only clue to his thoughts.

Chapter 2

Teltrena shivered as she descended into the Sandleyr; for some reason on that particular day, the inside of the Sandleyr seemed unnaturally cold compared to the outside. Normally the temperature was warmer, especially in the center of the Sandleyr, the Invitation Hall, where Onizards met to socialize and spread the latest gossip before returning to individual leyrs through the ledges that lined the cavernous walls of the Invitation Hall. In one of these leyrs rested Deybralfi, called the Fire Queen due to her sharp, biting hatred as much as her status as a Child of Fire. When Teltrena arrived there, she knew that the nice, cool temperature would vanish.

As she landed on the floor of the Invitation Hall, Teltrena did her best to ignore the Onizards who were staring at her and saying things behind her back. Since she had been disowned by the Children of Earth, she was a non-nature, an outcast in the Sandleyr population, and thus she would never be able to speak to the other Onizards without earning cruel remarks and a lecture from the Fire Queen about staying in her proper place. Idenno was the only Onizard she could talk to without dealing with scrutiny, and he was not exactly the most uplifting Onizard to talk to about anything. He had been forced to be the Watchzard around the time Teltrena had become a non-nature, and he would often speak about either poor Lady Rulsaesan and her torment or some brother he had apparently lost in the past. She was not really interested in finding out more information on either subject; it was his business, and she had her own problems to deal with.

As Teltrena started walking toward the Fire Queen's leyr, she was not watching what was ahead of her, and consequently did not see the outstretched tail in front of her until she had already tripped over it and fallen to the ground. She winced in pain, attempted to get back up again and realized in terror that she had injured herself to the point of needing healing. When she was still a Child of Earth, this was not a problem, but now she was forbidden from using her powers of healing. She was completely helpless and at the mercy of whoever happened to be nearby.

The other Onizard was a real Child of Earth, and she began to laugh at Teltrena's predicament. *Silly, clumsy non-nature! Look at the terrific mess that you've made on the floor of the Invitation Hall; what terrible luck when eggs are so close to hatching. Now I'll have to heal you, since you're too stupid to do it yourself.*

Teltrena hid her head in her wings from embarrassment as she heard more Onizards gathering around and laughing. Why couldn't they just leave her in peace?

I suggest you do heal her immediately, and apologize for tripping the young lady, said a male voice Teltrena did not recognize.

Strangely enough, the laughter died more quickly than it had started, and the Child of Earth obeyed his commands quickly and without question.

Now apologize to the lady, the voice commanded as if its owner had some grand authority in the Sandleyr.

Teltrena shuddered, waiting for the Child of Earth to retaliate against the boy for his stupidity. But that retaliation did not come; the Child of Earth quickly muttered a half-hearted apology to Teltrena before beating her wings loudly and heavily as she flew away.

You don't have to be afraid anymore, miss, said Teltrena's unexpected rescuer. *I suppose they'll be gossiping more about me than about you now.*

Teltrena uncovered her eyes and saw a Child of Fire with dark orange-red skin. He standing near enough to protect her from any further attacks, but thankfully far enough to give her plenty of her own space and not start unpleasant rumors. He surveyed her with his brown eyes as if he had a genuine sense of concern for her well-being, and he was smiling at Teltrena as if seeing her brought something good to his day. This kind of attention was new to her; she wasn't quite sure how to react.

Umm...thank you for your help, sir.

You're welcome. I cannot stand bullies, he said. *It was a pleasure, Miss...?*

Teltrena the non-nature, she sighed. Here would come the part where he realized his mistake and backed away slowly.

Ah, I had heard of you, but hadn't had the pleasure of meeting you, the boy said as he bowed. *I am Delbralfi.*

Teltrena choked back a cry of complete shock and embarrassment. *Lord Delbralfi, as in the son of the Fire Queen? I-I had no idea.*

Please, just Delbralfi, he said, as if his true title shamed him. *Being a Queen's son is not as honorable as everyone thinks it is, especially since the next Child of Light could appear at any moment and take away my mother's grand title.*

You believe in the next Child of Light? Teltrena gasped. Before the Fire Queen, the Children of Light had ruled the Sandleyr. They had been just if for no other reason than their ability to sense the emotions, including pain, of those around them. There were supposed to be two to rule the Day Kingdom and two to rule the Night, yet when the last Day Leyrque, Ammasan, had died, no one had inherited her powers. No one could know who the heir of Light was supposed to be until their powers manifested, and after ten years of waiting most had given up on the idea.

You mean to tell me you do not? Delbralfi asked. *Lady Rulsaesan still lives waiting for Ammasan's heir to help her rule. You would make her unhappy if she knew.*

You would make your mother unhappy if she knew you were hoping for her to lose her power, Teltrena said. She knew the Fire Queen was glad to boss all of the Onizards and humans around.

I have no mother, Delbralfi said a little too firmly. *But enough of that; I suppose she's heard of this incident by now, and I wouldn't want you to get in further trouble. Have a pleasant day, Teltrena non-nature.*

You too, she said, bowing to him before making a hasty retreat toward the Fire Queen's leyr, which suddenly seemed safer than where she was at the moment. She was rather happy that Delbralfi had saved her from further embarrassment, but at the same time confused, almost disturbed that he had actually taken the time to protect her and speak to her. She wasn't complaining, but noble Onizard men usually didn't bother to talk to her.

Teltrena dismissed thoughts of Delbralfi as she walked up to the large leyr that was inhabited by the Fire Queen. Before Teltrena could call out to her, the large Child of Fire exited on her own. Her crimson eyes, which stood out from her dark orange body, were formed into a glare that was further emphasized by the hideous scar under her left eye. Her tail lashed back and forth in frustration as she surveyed the area around her. Teltrena did her best to avoid looking at the scar, and became distracted by a human girl who was exiting the leyr quickly.

The fact that a human had escaped the Fire Queen's leyr unharmed was amazing; the Queen had a rather disturbing habit of killing random humans in the Sandleyr. She got away with it, since she was Queen and human beings had less status than even a powerless Onizard like Teltrena. The non-nature knew that she should not have cared what the Fire Queen did for amusement, as long as it didn't involve harassing her. But the thought that she was serving a creature who could take lives without any qualms whatsoever greatly disturbed Teltrena and made her wish for the days of the past when the Children of Light ruled the Sandleyr.

"Have a nice day, Miss Child of Earth," the girl said, her brown eyes meeting Teltrena's eyes. She smiled quickly before running off, presumably to return to her chores.

Completely baffled at the second smile of the day, and wondering if the brown-eyed creatures of the Sandleyr had all gone insane, Teltrena replied, *I am not a Child of Earth, little slave.*

The girl was long gone, though, and Teltrena did not have time to ponder the strangeness of a human girl who talked to random Onizards cheerfully, even after spending time with the Fire Queen.

I see you have discovered the daughter of a troublemaker, The Fire Queen sneered, startling Teltrena back to the present state of affairs. *It is nearly impossible to destroy that child's cheerful attitude, but I don't want to lose a worker who is actually efficient. My son's leyr is easily one of the largest in the Sandleyr, yet this mere human could clean it in a day!*

The child is cheerful even to you? Teltrena asked, more incredulously than perhaps was proper.

Yes, she is cheerful even when she thinks I am not watching her, so I know she is not faking it to please me, the Fire Queen replied, seemingly unaware of Teltrena's breach of etiquette. *That is a mystery that baffles me. I cannot understand what makes her so cheerful, but I have to put a stop to it. We can't have the humans getting above their station, after all.*

No, perhaps not, Teltrena sighed.

Perhaps not? You will do well to remember your own station, non-nature.

Yes, my queen, Teltrena said quickly, tightening her wings against her side even more. The Fire Queen was still in a relatively good mood; she didn't want to be called worse names than non-nature. *The Watchzard reports a storm coming to the Sandleyr, but all is well otherwise.*

A storm? The Fire Queen cringed as she hid her tail beneath her body. *I suppose I shall have to wait until the rain subsides before I investigate the Watchzard's condition myself. Hopefully the fool will take cover from the rain before he gets the urge to start that ridiculous dance of his. Tell me, how did he look?*

I'm not sure what you mean, my queen.

I mean exactly what I said, the Fire Queen said in the calm, slow tone she maintained when she was slightly annoyed. *How did the Watchzard look? What was his demeanor?*

You wish for the truth, my queen?

Yes, she said impatiently. *I cannot govern this Sandleyr based on lies, can I?*

He seemed miserable, my queen, Teltrena stated, carefully avoiding an answer to the last question.

For the first time in the conversation, the Fire Queen smiled. *Excellent. You are dismissed for now, non-nature.*

Chapter 3

Jena ran quickly up the path to her friend Delbralfi's leyr, hoping to celebrate with the Onizard when she arrived. Another day of escaping the Fire Queen's leyr unharmed was a cause for great glee in her circle of friends, though she knew it was only a matter of time before the Onizard Queen started asking her annoying and dangerous questions again. They were annoying because she had to pretend to be cheerful to the murderer of many of her fellow humans; they were dangerous because one wrong word, one frown, or one misplaced smile could make Jena one of the murdered.

Jena didn't like pretending to be cheerful, but she knew that it was the only way she would stay alive. Right now, the Fire Queen was confused about her, even curious; once that curiosity was gone, Jena knew her death would be hopefully swift, probably prolonged, and most assuredly painful.

As Jena reached the entrance to Delbralfi's leyr, Alair, her pet Onizac ran out to meet her. This caused her considerable worry, considering a human owning an Onizac was illegal in the Sandleyr. She hadn't asked to own Alair, though; she had simply been walking to her chore assignment two years ago when she noticed that a small, tan, fuzzy kitten with a sharp spike on his tail had begun to follow her. It wasn't until later, when Alair started speaking to her telepathically, that she realized that he was part of a Sandleyrian race of cats known as the Onizac, and that he had Bonded with her. In other words, he had all the usual quirks of the barn cats she had grown up with as well as the ability to scream in her head for food. Why the Onizards would want to hoard them was beyond her.

"Alair, get back into Delbralfi's leyr, you silly kitten!" Jena whispered.

Jena's back, the meanfire didn't bother her! squeaked Alair as he scampered back into Delbralfi's leyr.

It is good to see you back, Delbralfi added as Jena entered the leyr herself. *I'm glad that my demon mother didn't harm you.*

"It is good to be back," Jena said. "And it's still awful hearing you call her a demon, even if she is one. At least you have a mother, a mother who could still turn to good in spite of everything she's done."

The Fire Queen doesn't have any maternal instinct at all; why should I see her as a mother when she does not treat me like I am her son? But enough talk of her. I am trying to figure out why I am having strange but wonderful dreams recently about a Lady of Fire. Delbralfi said, smiling as he closed his eyes. *Even the memory of them is pleasant to me.*

"Isn't your mother the Lady of Fire?" Jena asked, "I don't see how that would be a pleasant dream."

That is one of the titles she claims, but the Lady of Fire that was in my dream wasn't the Fire Queen. She was much more like the mother I would have wanted, had I been given the choice. She was gentle, and if she were a human I think she would have sang to me. As it was, I was very small, and she cradled me in her tail and rocked me back and forth as a mother would rock her egg. She wasn't harsh and hot-tempered like the Fire Queen; her warmth was in her kindness. Then in the dream the sun began to rise, and though her eyes remained always on me, she seemed sad, almost like she was about to cry. She said, Good morning, *and that's when I woke up.*

"That does sound wonderful," Jena said. "I'm sorry you had to wake up, Delbralfi."

Don't be; it was only a dream. There's no need to put any more thought into it than that. The Child of Fire shrugged, as if trying to dismiss a thought that wouldn't leave his mind. *Besides, I was able to help an Onizard in need. She was being tormented by a Child of Earth for some unknown reason; the tormentor was saying something about her being too stupid to heal herself, as if being a non-nature is supposed to make someone stupid. Perhaps it was simply jealousy, because she didn't seem stupid to me. She was rather...well, never mind,* he ended lamely, avoiding eye contact.

"I did overhear a Child of Earth plotting some cruel prank against someone when I was on my way to the Fire Queen's leyr."

I stepped in and rescued her, then told her I believe the Children of Light would return, he said. *How stupid is that?*

"If you had reason to trust her, and you thought she was in trouble, it wasn't stupid at all. It was sweet."

It won't help me keep up my reputation as a dangerous brute, which I need to continue my work. I can't stop my mother on my own, but I can stop the lesser bullies just by showing my face, Delbralfi paused, as if remembering something. *Her name was Teltrena.*

"That would explain why she was late meeting the Fire Queen. That demon was angry and grumbling about the non-nature; it was why I was able to get out so quickly."

The poor girl! I am sorry to have delayed her further. No one deserves the torment of the Fire Queen.

"I really feel sorry for Teltrena; she's stuck listening to the Fire Queen and running errands for her all day. I doubt the crime she committed against the Sandleyr to earn her status was enough to deserve that."

I doubt anyone deserves that; I pity the poor girl, Delbralfi agreed, sighing. *Well, I hope the parts of your day that didn't involve the Fire Queen have been going well, Jena.*

"My day has been going wonderfully. I managed to trick the Fire Queen into letting me continue to be the official human that takes care of you and Alair."

She still thinks Alair belongs to me? Delbralfi suppressed his laughter. *I don't see how she could believe that; I've rarely ever left my leyr these past few years for enough time that an Onizac kitten would find me.*

"Well, she does, and as long as she does, Alair and I are still safe. That's what's important."

Indeed.

As they spoke, a voice from the center of the Invitation Hall called out, *The Watchzard reports a storm coming. It is less than three flights away, so be prepared, Children of Fire.*

Lovely, muttered Delbralfi. *I just hope Rulsaesan's eggs are safe. Then again, I suppose if they are Children of Water like their father it will not matter.*

"Babies in the Sandleyr will be so wonderful, Delbralfi. There haven't been any, human or Onizard, for a long time," Jena said.

Not since I was born, Delbralfi added. *It will be a nice change to be one of the older Onizards instead of the hatchling of the Sandleyr. Five children; Rulsaesan and Deyraeno must be proud. Perhaps there will even be a Bonding!*

Jena smiled at the possibility. From what the Onizards had told her, whenever Onizard eggs hatched, the father would order all of the unBonded Onizards to the Invitation Hall and with the help of his unhatched children he would choose those he thought worthy of Bonding one of his children. This was called the Inviting ceremony, and it was what gave the Invitation Hall its name. Those chosen were called the Invited, and they would fly outside to the tall sandstone structure called the Leyr Grounds. That was where the eggs were located, and that was where a Bonding would occur.

When an Onizard Bonded, they were instantly linked to their Bond in mind and senses. It was, Jena was told, something like Bonding an Onizac, but it went much deeper than merely having something follow your around. Bonds were said to sense in their Bond what a Child of Light sensed in all creatures; when one Bond died, the other died as well. Few Onizards actually Bonded, so nearly everyone in the Sandleyr respected a Bonded Onizard.

Don't forget what it means to Bond an Onizac, Jena, Delbralfi added, bringing her back to the present.

"I know," Jena said with a sigh, "Onizacs were a gift from the great Leyrkan Senbralni to teach true tolerance, and every Onizard that has Bonded an Onizac has eventually Bonded another Onizard. But I'm not an Onizard, unless I'm really an Onizard with only two legs and no tail or wings."

Perhaps you're not an Onizard, but think about it, Jena! Delbralfi said excitedly. *If a human were to Bond an Onizard, it would prove to my mother that the humans are equal to us! And before you say she'll kill the human that Bonds, if she did that she would be killing the Onizard as well, and that is a crime that would strip her of her title. She wouldn't dare kill an Onizard.*

"Perhaps you're right, but I'm no heroic Bond of anyone."

Suddenly, someone emitted a loud, jubilant cry that echoed throughout the Sandleyr.

"What was that?"

I'm not sure, Delbralfi answered, stepping closer to the entrance of his leyr. *It sounded like a crazy person.*

All Bond-worthy are to report to the Invitation Hall immediately, a loud voice boomed from outside. *The Lady Rulsaesan's children are hatching.*

Come on, Jena, that's us, Delbralfi said as he turned to his friend.

"But if I go out there, and the Fire Queen finds out-" Jena stammered.

I'll say that I forced you to go out there out of nervousness. Besides, why throw away an opportunity like this? It's not like you'll be noticed with all the Onizards out there anyway.

"Well, if you say so, I'll go," Jena said. "Alair, guard the leyr for us."

I'll guard well for Jena, no meanfires here, Alair said before stretching lazily.

Then let's get going! Delbralfi exclaimed, running outside before suddenly coming to a halt.

As Jena reached the entrance, she could see why her friend had stopped; the entire Invitation Hall was covered with Onizards, and Delbralfi's ledge was the only free spot available to the two of them. Glancing about, Jena discovered that Deyraeno was walking about along the edge of the Invitation Hall.

Deyraeno had a stare like the intensity of a powerful wave; once caught in it, few could resist both respecting and fearing his gaze while it remained on them. The way he bore his wings as he walked about made him seem like a tall and stately human prince clothed in indigo. He did not utter a word to the masses, but whenever he stopped to Invite an Onizard they seemed to get his message; occasionally, Jena would hear an Onizard cry out in delight and fly up toward the entrance. Every time this happened, Deyraeno's pace seemed more urgent than before, and those around him appeared even more nervous.

He's Invited two so far, Delbralfi said.

"Three," Jena corrected as a Child of Earth flew toward the entrance.

He's headed straight for us, Delbralfi informed her nervously.

They halted their conversation as Deyraeno, indeed, appeared to be walking straight toward them. Jena became terrified when she realized all of the Onizards were looking at her. Despite what Delbralfi said, she feared for her life. After all, Delbralfi was sometimes wrong about how his mother would react to his clever lies.

Deyraeno stared at Delbralfi and Jena for a moment. It was not a cold stare, but a stare of one in a moment of decision. Suddenly, he grinned, and Jena wondered if it was a good thing that the other Onizards were watching.

Delbralfi and Jena, shouted Deyraeno to the crowd, shocking everyone when they realized what he was sharing with them, *you are Invited.*

Chapter 4

Deyraeno was worried, but he tried to hide it. He could not disapprove of his son's choice to Invite Jena the human, but at the same time he feared what this would mean for the future of his family. He did not want the birth of his children to gain more attention than was necessary. They were already destined for unneeded recognition due to their mother's status as last of the Day Children; to have a human Invited would cause them a ridiculous amount of teasing and shame, even though she was not even likely to Bond. The majority of Onizards did not understand that human beings were no different intellectually from Onizards. Deyraeno considered them superior in many ways to his own kind, but simply because she walked on two legs instead of four, Jena was certain to die unless Deyraeno could find some way to protect her.

"What?" the girl cried. Deyraeno could tell she was aware of the danger she faced, for she seemed more fearful than happy at the Invitation. "Can humans actually Bond?" she asked, her voice softer as she actually began to sound hopeful. The Child of Water knew she was only asking that question to make the other Onizards use their brains. She was smiling bravely and appeared ready to go.

As he looked at the girl's dark red hair and brown eyes, Deyraeno was suddenly reminded of another human he once knew. Though she had been older than Jena, she had the same look of determination and hope as she went into the Fire Queen's leyr and never came out again. He had failed to protect her then, but he would not let the same fate happen to Jena. *We shall see,* he said calmly. *Delbralfi, feel free to go to the Leyr Grounds. I will convey Jena there myself.*

Yes sir, said Delbralfi, bowing awkwardly before turning to fly away. *Good luck, Jena.*

"Good luck, Delbralfi," Jena whispered, worried that this was one of the last times she would ever speak to her friend.

She did not doubt that all would work out for the best in the end, but she worried that in the short run things would turn out badly for them.

Climb onto my tail, Jena, Deyraeno commanded, lifting his tail up to the ledge for her to obey his order. *The Fire Queen will not get anywhere near you if I have anything to say about it,* he added, and from the way he glanced about the Invitation Hall, Jena sensed that he had spoken privately to her.

Jena smiled weakly, put some trust in the Child of Water, and stepped onto his tail. Deyraeno waited for her to steady herself before he lifted her carefully onto his back. It felt strange being lifted in the air like this, especially with so many Onizards watching her. She feared she would make a fool out of herself, but she managed to keep herself from falling, and Deyraeno smiled at her reassuringly.

When Jena was carefully situated on his back, Deyraeno called out, *All have been Invited!* Then he spread his wings and leapt into the air.

Jena gripped on tightly at first, and she tried not to look at the ground for fear of falling. After Deyraeno got airborne, however, she began to like the feeling of flight. She saw the Onizards below as little as they had called her and she laughed in spite of the situation.

You'll find things are much different once you've gone above the entrance, Deyraeno explained. *It is a place few Onizards go, so it is much quieter than the Invitation Hall. Though I suppose with the storm coming it will be louder than usual.*

Jena could not remember what a storm was like, so she was curious about what he meant. As Deyraeno exited the Sandleyr, she noticed the dark sky overhead and shivered from the unexpected cold.

"I thought it was supposed to be warmer outside," Jena said.

But Deyraeno was not paying attention; he had paused his flight for the moment to bow his head to a Child of Water sitting on a large rock nearby. Jena assumed he was the Watchzard, and had to wonder why Deyraeno was bowing, the Onizards' highest way of showing honor, to an Onizard of little importance. But soon he was flying away, and Jena's attention turned to the tower in front of them. The aged sandstone seemed venerable and trustworthy, and from this angle the bowl at the top seemed almost as big as the caverns below them. Jena couldn't help but gasp at the sight.

Behold the Leyr Grounds, Deyraeno said, *where every Onizard has hatched since Senbralni's time.*

The Leyr Grounds were larger that she remembered them, but the last time she had seen them she had been in the distance just arriving at the Sandleyr for the first time. Her family had been part of a village raided for more human workers, and at the time she had been too worried that she was going to be killed by her kidnappers to notice how large the Leyr Grounds truly were. But this time the Leyr Grounds seemed to be beckoning her to go higher and see what was on the other side.

Deyraeno finally soared over the Leyr Grounds wall and landed by the Invited, and after he carefully set her down on the ground again she began to examine her surroundings.

The first thing Jena noticed was Rulsaesan, the mother of the eggs. She was hard to miss, as her skin had a vibrant saffron glow, and on the end of her tail was a bright orb that lit up the entire Leyr Grounds. The orb symbolized that she was a Child of Light, and if she had her proper title, she would be called Leyrque, the heart of the Sandleyr and true ruler of the Onizards. But when the former Leyrque died under mysterious circumstances, no Onizard gained the form of a Child of Light and, since Rulsaesan could not control her powers of ultimate empathy alone, the Fire Queen had taken over the Sandleyr.

Rulsaesan still appeared more regal than the other Onizards, now that Jena saw her up close for the first time. While the other Onizards had the same three horns, two curved over their head and one formed straight toward the sky, hers seemed like a magnificent crown of gold. Her grey eyes drifted among the Invited, pausing only a moment on Jena before she smiled and moved on.

Jena quickly took her mind off Rulsaesan, however, and focused on the rocking eggs. Each of them seemed special to her, but she could not decide which egg she thought was the best. After a few moments of indecision, she wondered if she was guilty of some crime for trying to decide which egg was the best when she did not truly belong there in the first place.

Jena! Delbralfi called out excitedly, walking over to her. *Isn't this great?*

"Wonderful," Jena said distractedly.

Delbralfi happened to glance up at the sky and suddenly appeared nervous. *Well, it is great that you and I are both Invited, but not so great if that weather doesn't clear up.*

"Huh?" Jena said, glancing up to see what Delbralfi meant. Seeing the storm clouds again, she remembered the threat the rain posed to Children of Fire like her friend. "It doesn't look pretty up there. I hope the weather holds until you've Bonded, Delbralfi."

You really think I'll Bond? Delbralfi asked.

"I know you will," Jena said. Glancing past Delbralfi, she added, "But maybe you should look behind you; one of the eggs has hatched."

Delbralfi turned about to see a baby Child of Water cleaning his tail. His skin was almost the same color as his father's skin, but when he looked up Jena could see that everything else about him, including his gray eyes, resembled Rulsaesan. Delbralfi stared dumbfounded for several long seconds. *Deldenno?*

The hatchling nodded and smiled.

Deldenno! Delbralfi exclaimed, laughing in delight as he ran to him and lifted the young Child of Water. *Jena, you were right. Meet Deldenno, my Bond.*

Jena thought she heard Deyraeno snickering as he watched from his place beside Rulsaesan, but she assumed it was just her imagination. "A pleasure to meet you, Deldenno. I suppose you and your Bond will wish to escape the storm now."

I will, at any rate, said Delbralfi. *I sense many fights over that in the future. But for now, we are content to wait inside until we meet you and your Bond.*

"If you say so," Jena said. "Good-bye, Delbralfi and Deldenno."

Good-bye! The Child of Fire answered back as he flew away.

A few minutes after Delbralfi and Deldenno left, the storm clouds opened up and rain began to pour over the Sandleyr. Jena had to hold her hand over her eyes at times to see clearly, but this did not bother her. She could not remember ever seeing or feeling rain, and it was a pleasant experience for her. During this time, two female hatchlings emerged from their eggs. One, a Child of Earth, announced her name as Amsaena; the other, a Child of Water, declared the name Rulraeno proudly. Jena watched Rulsaesan carefully lift them both onto her back before turning her attention to the last two eggs.

As Jena watched a small Child of Water emerge from his egg, his soft blue eyes held her attention until a large part of the old wall, knocked lose by the rain, began to fall toward him.

Dey! cried Rulsaesan in horror.

I've got it, dear, assured her mate, blasting a jet stream of water toward the falling wall. If the falling wall had stayed solid as it flew away in the opposite direction, his tactic would have worked, but a small part of the wall broke off from the rest and fell onto the leg of the hatchling. The child let out a cry of pain that made all on the Leyr Grounds shudder, especially Jena.

No! screamed Rulsaesan as she winced from the pain her son was feeling.

Leave him! shouted Deyraeno to a Child of Earth that had begun to run toward the hatchling. *As much as I regret it, the Fire Queen ordered long ago that any injured hatchling cannot be rescued from the Leyr Grounds unless it Bonds.*

Jena fought tears as she realized that they were going to leave the hatchling to die, but she suddenly felt ice cold rainwater surrounding her. "Why is the water getting higher?"

There is too much rain; the Leyr Grounds cannot take it, Rulsaesan said. *Quickly! Everyone leave before the smaller of us drown!*

Jena debated running toward Deyraeno, but stopped when she realized that in the confusion, everyone had ignored the last hatchling, a Child of Wind. He was already in water close to his neck, and he was desperately trying to get toward the shallower water near Jena. Quickly, she ran out until the water was deep enough to swim in, then swam the remaining distance to him. "Don't worry, I'll get you to safety," she said as she grabbed the hatchling with one arm and swam toward the shallows with the other. It was extremely difficult, for though the hatchling should have known Jena was saving his life, he still cried in terror and attempted to fight for freedom from Jena's gentle grasp until they reached the shallows, where the Child of Earth was waiting for him.

I am eternally in debt to you for saving Delculble, she said with a bow. There was amazement and gratitude in her expression, as if Jena were the last creature she'd expect to rescue her Bond. Then she turned and flew away, leaving only Jena, Rulsaesan, Deyraeno, and the injured hatchling.

Rulsaesan turned her head toward her son, and avoided eye contact with Deyraeno as she said, *Do not worry, Senraeno. Things will work out, and Uncle Iden will protect you.*

"Who is Uncle Iden?" Jena asked Deyraeno, who was closer to her.

What are you talking about? Deyraeno asked.

"Rulsaesan just said Uncle Iden would protect Senraeno."

Rulsaesan did not say anything, unless she was speaking privately to her son, Deyraeno said, concern filling his mental voice.

Jena blinked in surprise. Why had she heard Rulsaesan when her mate did not?

Climb onto my tail again, Jena, Deyraeno said. *The ceremony is over.*

Jena stepped onto Deyraeno's tail, but she hesitated when it came time for her to climb back onto his back so that they could leave. Rulsaesan had meant her words for her son alone, and yet Jena had heard them as clearly as if Rulsaesan had been speaking directly to her. She felt embarrassed that she had been listening to a private conversation, and she felt terrible for claiming to be against the Fire Queen while letting an innocent die without aid due to the Fire Queen's orders.

Jena! a small yet persistent, urgent voice cried. Jena was suddenly aware of both a tingling sensation in her head and a sharp pain in her leg.

"Deyraeno, did you just call my name?" Jena asked. As soon as she uttered the words, however, she felt stupid for asking.

No, the adult Onizard replied. *Why are you still standing on my tail?*

Jena! The hatchling cried again, this time more urgently than before; the water was almost above his head. Tears filled his eyes as he added, *Don't leave me behind. I chose you.*

"I'm coming, Senraeno!" Jena answered suddenly, diving into the water to save him.

If she had looked back, she would have seen a dumbfounded expression on Deyraeno's face. But Jena did not look back as she swam with all her might toward Senraeno. With every stroke she fought for her life and the life of her Bond. When she reached him, she saw the blood in the water around them and briefly felt the panic in Senraeno's heart joining her own fear for their safety. Wasn't it all fruitless anyway, when they didn't have the support of Senraeno's parents?

Dismissing those thoughts for the moment, Jena dove underneath the water and carefully removed the rock that covered his leg, freeing Senraeno to swim with three of his legs on the surface.

We will go now? Senraeno asked. *I'm scared.*

"Don't fear," Jena said as she reminded herself how to tread water. "We'll find a place that isn't scary. You just need to trust me."

Sure, Senraeno said. *I'll always trust my Jena.*

As the pair prepared to swim back to where Deyraeno had been, Jena saw nothing but the opposite wall and more water. She fought the panic coming over both her and Senraeno until the older Onizard picked them both up with his tail and placed them onto his back.

That was an unnecessary risk of your life, Jena, Deyraeno scolded. *Even before I learned he was your Bond, I was going to walk over and pick up Senraeno myself as soon as you were safely on my back.*

Jena managed to blush from embarrassment as she tried to keep her mind away from the cold, wet clothing on her skin. "But...you said..."

I lied, he said, before beginning to laugh. *If you seriously thought that I'd leave my child here to die, you know nothing of being a parent. You will learn, though, before the end comes. As his Bond, you're going to have to be a second mother to him.*

"So you tricked everyone into thinking you would leave him so you could hide him?"

Yes, Deyraeno said as he left the Leyr Grounds. *When you were Invited, I was planning on hiding only you, but the hiding place I know of has room for Senraeno as well. But please, the next time you plan on doing something that crazy, warn me first.*

"I will," Jena said as she laughed.

Don't worry, Zarder Jena, I will protect you someday, when I'm bigger, Senraeno said.

"Zarder?" Jena asked, blinking at the unfamiliar word.

Deyraeno laughed. *He called you Zarder? It sounds like a cross between 'Onizard' and 'erstai', the Onizaran word for human. I guess he's calling you a two-legged Onizard.*

Jena giggled at the explanation in spite of fears about the future. It didn't sound like too bad of a title; Zarder Jena, human Bond of the Onizard Senraeno. She had a feeling that the Sandleyr would be a different place once she and Senraeno had grown up.

Chapter 5

Jena shivered from the cold and the pain she felt in her leg through her link to her Bond, but she was still happy to be alive as Deyraeno slowly returned to the Sandleyr. The only worry that had disappeared was the rain, which had lessened significantly. "How are we going to get a Child of Earth to help Senraeno without the Fire Queen finding out about us?"

That is one of the many questions that I am pondering, Deyraeno said. *The most important question now is how I will explain this to Watchzard Idenno. He's dealing with enough issues of his own without having to worry about how to take care of two renegades.*

"Besides, he might tell the Fire Queen about us."

Deyraeno guffawed. *Idenno would never betray anyone to the Fire Queen, much less a son of his two closest friends. He saved our lives long ago, and he is the only Onizard I'd trust with this secret. The only reason I won't tell him is because I don't want him worrying about you two. As I said, he has issues of his own to worry about.*

"I suppose I'll have to believe you're right about him," Jena said. "Maybe you can hold your wings up so that no one could see us while you're talking to him."

That could work, Deyraeno mused. *Yes, I believe that is the safest course of action.*

Is that the Watchzard down there? Senraeno asked as he glanced downward. *He doesn't seem to be worrying.*

Jena looked down and laughed. Watchzard Idenno was dancing in the middle of the storm. With extravagant steps and leaps Idenno pranced about the entrance of the Sandleyr, each movement seeming more graceful and carefully planned than the last. Then suddenly he stopped. For a long, awkward moment he stood still. Then, with his wings lowered, he walked back to the Watchzard rock.

"That's odd," Jena commented.

Don't make fun of Idenno, Deyraeno said abruptly. *He has been through a rougher time than almost any other Onizard in this Sandleyr. Each step brings him joy for a moment, but the pain when he hits the ground again takes that joy away from him.*

"I wasn't going to make fun of him," Jena said, before Deyraeno landed and she had to remain silent.

Deyraeno, please don't tell me you left them up there! Idenno exclaimed. *I will rescue them myself if you did!*

I did, Deyraeno said. *But only because they were dead.*

You fool! That was your son! screamed Idenno. Even though Jena could not see him, she could hear him sobbing and knew he was greatly distressed. *You coward! How are you going to face Rulsaesan? Why didn't you ask for my help the second you knew something was wrong? Was the help of a washed-out Watchzard not good enough for you?* In a fit of rage and grief, he pushed Deyraeno, causing him to stumble backwards and nearly drop Jena and Senraeno.

Iden, calm yourself! Deyraeno exclaimed.

Calm myself? Your son is dead, and it's your fault!

It will be my fault, if they don't believe me! Deyraeno admitted as he lowered his wings to reveal Jena and Senraeno very much alive.

Idenno's show of anger instantly ceased. *Dey, are they...?*

Yes, he said, before losing his composure and sobbing. *I'm so scared, Iden.*

You have no reason to be, the Watchzard said, his mental voice changed to calm and comforting tone. *I made a promise to Rulsaesan long ago, and I intend to keep it. As long as I'm still breathing, the Fire Queen will not harm your family. I'll even go knock down the rest of that old section of the wall to make everyone think the two of them were buried underneath the rubble. The Fire Queen will have no choice but to believe the Watchzard,* he added with a smile.

Thank you, Iden, Deyraeno said, taking several deep breaths before continuing with, *you have been a better friend than we deserve. When our children have grown old enough to hear the tale, we will tell them of the true heroes of the Sandleyr.*

Nonsense, Deyraeno; when they are old enough, I will tell them myself. You don't seriously think I'd neglect Delden and his siblings, do you? Idenno laughed for the first time in the conversation. *I find it extremely ironic that he Bonded Delbralfi. He looks like his mother, you know.*

Really? I did not notice. Delden wasn't really paying attention to me, you know.

Idenno shrugged. *Ah, the youth ignoring their older and wiser parents for their friends. It starts at an early age, from what I was told growing up. But it seems the two of them are as happy as they can be, and that is what is important. In the meantime, go find a safe spot to hide your son and his Bond. What were your names, anyway?* he asked as he turned to Jena. *I am sorry for ignoring you, but circumstances such as they are, Daddy Dey here needed my attention first.*

"We are Jena and Senraeno. Thank you for your help, Watchzard Idenno."

I am Senraeno, Senraeno added, *and like you, I wish to speak of myself by myself. Thank you.*

Idenno smiled. *It's no problem at all; I'm glad to help a child of Rulsaesan and Deyraeno, and you seem like a nice human from the few seconds I've talked to you, Jena. It seems you're just as stubborn as your parents, Senraeno. I'm sure you will go far in life, as soon as your father figures out what to do. Which I'm sure is a tough job for him, given the mess you've gotten him into.*

Indeed, said Deyraeno. *For now, we face a new dilemma. How are we going to help Senraeno's injured leg?*

The Fire Queen wishes for a report from the Watchzard, Teltrena said in a monotone voice as she flew out of the main entrance. When she saw the group that had gathered, she gasped and shouted, *What is going on?*

I believe I know just the Child of Earth who can fix your leg, Senraeno, Idenno said, as they all turned to look at her.

Chapter 6

Teltrena stared at the scene in front of her in complete confusion. She did not understand why Deyraeno was carrying an injured hatchling and a human girl on his back, for she had skipped the Invitation ceremony entirely. After all, she was a mere non-nature, and so she had no chance of being Invited anyway. Rumors said that a hatchling had died in the chaos of returning to the Sandleyr, but the wind and rain seemed to be calmer now. It seemed that honorable Deyraeno was breaking the Fire Queen's law, and a renegade human was involved. Teltrena became even more confused when she realized that the human was the young girl she had seen earlier. The only thing she was certain about was the terror she felt from the implications of what Idenno said. *I cannot help you. I am not a Child of Earth.*

You certainly expressed a desire to be one earlier, Idenno commented wryly.

But I...the child was supposed to be left on the Leyr Grounds because he didn't Bond, Teltrena stammered. She became even more confused when this was only greeted by laughter from the other four.

"We are Bonds."

I am Bonded, Senraeno explained at the same time.

You mean that a human has actually Bonded an Onizard? Teltrena asked carefully.

Yes! the other Onizards said at once.

Teltrena could tell she was being a nuisance again, and so she fell silent.

Teltrena, you must swear that you will not tell anyone, Idenno said. *This is a matter of life and death for two Bonds.*

I will tell no one, Teltrena promised. *Who would believe me, anyway?*

The Fire Queen would, Deyraeno said. *She will take such a claim seriously, because it is a threat to the authority she gains when others accept the beliefs under which she rules.*

"Yes, you may not be able to call a human 'little slave' much longer once word gets out that we are capable of Bonding," Jena said.

Teltrena blinked in surprise; she had not realized the girl had actually heard her. *I am sorry about that. There were a lot of things going through my mind, and it just slipped.*

You should be sorry, Idenno chided. *You called her a little slave? Why, you and I are slaves ourselves.*

Teltrena bowed her head in shame.

"There's no need to get defensive," Jena said. "I understand completely, Teltrena. You had to deal with the Fire Queen, and if you had actually called me a kind name, she would have been harsh on you. In the mean time, since the Fire Queen can't exactly come out here while it's raining, could you please help Senraeno? I don't know what you heard happened, but the leg injury at least was no rumor."

Teltrena eyed Senraeno's leg and frowned.

My son needs healing, or he will die from an infected wound, Deyraeno said. *It is your duty as a Child of Earth to heal without prejudice.*

Teltrena sighed. Deyraeno was correct; it was one of the highest laws of a Child of Earth law to heal without prejudice. However, since she was by decree of the Fire Queen a non-nature, those ethical laws did not apply to her, and she was terrified of being caught impersonating a Child of Earth. *But last time I tried to heal someone, I failed,* she protested. *I became a non-nature for a reason.*

Somehow I doubt that reason had anything to do with your abilities, Deyraeno said. *Before you became a non-nature, the Ladies of Earth were always telling Rulsaesan what a wonderful healer you were.*

Really? Teltrena asked, surprise that she had gotten such praise from the higher ranking Children of Earth. *Well, I suppose that was before I became a non-nature and a disgrace to the Sandleyr.*

"Please, Miss Teltrena, you are our only hope, a new voice said to Teltrena. When she realized it was Senraeno, she blinked in surprise. *I don't know what haunts you in your past, but Jena and I don't care. We trust you with our lives now.*

Teltrena smiled at the sign of respect from the young Onizard and made her decision. *Very well, I will heal him. But we must get him indoors, or else the rain will distract me.*

Idenno began to laugh uncontrollably. Between gasps for air, he managed to say, *Rain distracts a Child of Earth...more than three...Children of Water?*

We will meet in the abandoned leyr near the entrance, Deyraeno said, ignoring the Watchzard.

The Fire Queen's old leyr? Idenno asked as he finally managed to calm his laughter, *The irony is incredible. But it's a good idea; I don't think anyone ever goes there.*

They don't, Teltrena confirmed. *I sometimes go up there to think because no one will bother me there, not even the Fire Queen. But we can't all go at once; someone will suspect. I will tell the Fire Queen-*

That they were swept away when Jena tried to save the hatchling, Deyraeno finished.

"Please tell Delbralfi as well; Alair, my Onizac, is still in his care. But please be gentle when telling him the news; Deldenno, his new Bond, is his only other friend."

I will do as you have asked, Teltrena said, pondering many new things as she flew back into the Sandleyr.

Chapter 7

Delbralfi stood at the edge of his leyr, listening to the other Onizards speak rumors of death and destruction. He had told Deldenno to play with Alair, and the two of them were playing a game of Catch the Onizac, completely oblivious to the discussion outside the leyr. It was as Delbralfi wanted it; he did not want the two younger creatures worrying about what was going on. He worried enough on his own.

He did not notice the Onizard approaching until she was nearly beside him, and he became anxious when he realized it was the non-nature he had rescued earlier.
As the messenger, Teltrena had inside knowledge of the Sandleyr greater than that of the Fire Queen herself. He did not know whether to be glad she was there to clarify what had happened or to be afraid of what she had to say.

Deldenno and I greet you, he said as he bowed to her. *Come in, and bring your news. It is not often that I am asked to entertain a Child of Earth.*

I am no Child of Earth, she replied. *Though I thank you for your help earlier.*

You tail is shaped like a leaf, your skin is green, and you have lovely verdant eyes. I see a Child of Earth; I do not go by what my mother thinks.

Thank you, Teltrena said, casting her eyes to the ground. *I do not deserve your compliments, though; I am the bearer of bad news.*

What has happened? Is Jena okay?

Teltrena sighed and glanced over at Alair, who had run to the entrance of the leyr. *I am afraid your Onizac friend is unBonded.*

No! Delbralfi exclaimed as tears formed. *It's all my fault!*

I am sure it is not your fault, Delbralfi, Teltrena said. He could tell she was trying her best to console him, but nothing could help now. *She died with honor. You may have heard a hatchling was injured; this is true. She tried to save him, but they were both swept away before Deyraeno could get to them.*

Delbralfi could not speak amidst his sobs.

I will leave you in peace now, Teltrena said, her own voice wavering. *I am sorry.*

As Teltrena walked away, Alair began pawing at Delbralfi's feet.

I guess I'll have to take care of you while you still live, Alair. I'm sure that's what Jena would have wanted, as he noticed confusion in the Onizac's eyes, he added, *what is wrong, Alair?*

How did the nature lady know I'm Jena's Bond? Jena's not dead. Is Jena in trouble?

Chapter 8

I am here, Teltrena said as she entered the formerly abandoned leyr. As she looked around, though, it still seemed abandoned to her. The entire back of the leyr was concealed in shadows, and there was no noise except the sound of her cautious footsteps. She had to wonder if the renegades had even arrived yet.

Good, Deyraeno said, startling her as he emerged from the darkness. *I leave you two in Teltrena's care,* he said to the Bonds as he stepped toward the edge of the leyr. *Do not go near the edge unless it is absolutely necessary, and try to be awake at night and asleep during the day.* After he finished giving this warning, he opened his wings and began to glide toward the floor of the Invitation Hall.

He will have to go to the Fire Queen to report, Teltrena said as the two children emerged to watch Deyraeno leave. *I have no idea why he advised you to sleep during the day; I've heard a terrible duo of monstrous Onizards rules during the empty night. They can sense if you are awake, and strike without remorse at anything that dares to stay awake in their Night Kingdom. Sometimes Onizards can hear the terrible cries of Mad Mekanni, and the wrath of Delsenni is great toward...whoever it was that made her wrathful.*

"Where did you hear all of that silly nonsense, Teltrena?"

Come to think of it, the Onizard who told me this was the Fire Queen. When I was still young, she used to say it to me whenever she wanted to threaten me into doing my duties properly. One time, she actually forced me to stay awake briefly, and I did hear someone screaming. Teltrena halted her story as she realized what she was saying. There was often screaming when the Fire Queen was around; she should have known better than to scare the human and the small child with stories. *But don't let something like that keep you afraid of following*

Deyraeno's advice. I'm sure it's perfectly sound. Meanwhile, this seems to be a really nice place, she lied as she glanced at the various cobwebs and creepy shadows on the walls.

"Even if we're exiled here?" Jena began to laugh hysterically, and Teltrena had to smile in spite of the situation. "It seems more than acceptable, though, considering the circumstances. But I don't think we'll enjoy or hate it unless Senraeno's leg is better."

Of course, said Teltrena as she began to examine the wound. She muttered to herself when glancing at one part that had begun to bleed but smiled when she had finished. *It really isn't as bad as it looks, though I assume it must be dreadfully painful.*

"Yes, it is," said Jena, speaking on behalf of herself and Senraeno.

Well, it is fractured, but it is a simple thing for a Child of Earth to fix. Even a former Child of Earth should have no problem, Teltrena explained, holding her tail up in the air as its tip began to glow. *I'll need you both to hold still,* she cautioned before placing her tail gently on the wound.

Teltrena found that, even after so many years of neglecting her powers, she was able to heal the wound easily. She could see that both Jena and Senraeno were smiling in relief from the pain.

Then, for no explainable reason, Teltrena saw an image of Deyraeno and Jena in the distance. The water was surrounding him, and he feared Jena would never come to rescue him.

Jena! the hatchling cried.

Then at once she was back again in the abandoned leyr with Jena and Senraeno.

That Onizard with the frightening eyes...is she the Fire Queen? Senraeno asked.

Teltrena shifted uncomfortably. How had she seen what appeared to be Senraeno's memory? More importantly, what had Senraeno seen while she saw his memory? *Perhaps, but that isn't important now. Your leg is fine now, isn't it?*

Yes, Senraeno said. *It is as good as new, though technically my whole body is new anyway.*

Teltrena laughed in relief; she glad that the hatchling wasn't pursuing the subject further.

"Teltrena, what happened to Alair?"

Oh my...I left him down there in Delbralfi's leyr. I am sorry, Jena, I will retrieve him for you immediately.

All Onizards report to the Invitation Hall! a harsh voice shouted from below.

Never mind, Teltrena said with a sigh. *That was the Fire Queen; I'd recognize her voice anywhere. I will talk to Delbralfi about getting Alair as soon as I can,* Teltrena promised before flying down to join the other Onizards.

Chapter 9

Jena watched from above as all the humans that were out in the Invitation Hall ran for their lives; the Fire Queen was in the Invitation Hall now, and any human that shared the space with her when she called for the Onizards to report was as good as dead.

All Onizards report! she bellowed for a second time as she looked about at all that had assembled.

From above, Jena could see Delbralfi and Deldenno standing at the edge of their leyr. Delbralfi held his usual expressionless face that he wore in public, while Deldenno appeared to be confused about what was happening.

Deyraeno, shouted the Fire Queen, *we all know that your children have hatched, so give the new Bonded their brief moment of recognition so we can get on with our lives.*

Several of the Onizards became noticeably angry at the Fire Queen's disrespect for Bonded Onizards. Delbralfi and Deldenno stormed back into their leyr in disgust.

Deyraeno appeared angry as well, but as he stepped out to where the Fire Queen could see him, he hid his anger as best as he could. He glanced at Rulsaesan for a moment before saying, *The Sandleyr can welcome two new Bonds: Deldenno, Bond of Delbralfi,* he paused to look for the pair but when he could not find them, he continued, *and Delculble, Bond of Ransenna,* he paused again, but this time he actually found the pair; Ransenna seemed to be pondering something, while Delculble smiled shyly at the sudden attention.

Deyraeno nodded to the pair and continued with, *we also were blessed with two daughters; Amsaena and Rulraeno. We are thankful to be blessed with four healthy children, and look forward to watching them grow up and make the Sandleyr a better and more loving place.*

The Fire Queen laughed coldly as she said, *A more loving place? Love is overrated. Were there not five eggs, Deyraeno? Surely nothing could have happened to a child of Rulsaesan, last of the Children of Light!*

Jena frowned. "She's doing this to hurt your dad and mom," she whispered to Senraeno. "Teltrena already told her what happened."

Deyraeno looked toward the ground, avoiding the Fire Queen's glare. *I am sad to say one child perished, along with the human that was Invited.*

What did you expect? asked the Fire Queen. *You should know humans bring nothing but bad luck to the Sandleyr. The child was a weakling; we shall spend no more time mourning it, but we can rejoice that a human has perished.*

Rulsaesan, walking slowly toward her leyr, appeared to disagree.

The human had a name and a personality of her own, Deybralfi, Deyraeno said.

Mind your place, Deyraeno. The name Deybralfi is dead to me; I am the Fire Queen, and you owe me your respect.

Very well, Fire Queen, Deyraeno said. *I respect what authority the Sandleyr law has given you, but I do not owe any loyalty to your misguided beliefs. The Sandleyr should mourn the red-haired girl, the most powerful of the humans, because any death is worthy of the care of others.*

I do not see why anyone should care about a human's death, except that makes it even more excellent, the Fire Queen smiled. *That girl came from a line of traitors, and with her dies all of the opposition from the humans.*

"That is where you are wrong, Fire Queen!" a male voice shouted. "For as long as you live the humans will oppose you."

Who is that? Senraeno asked Jena.

Jena scanned the Invitation Hall until she saw the lone human walking toward the Fire Queen as if he had the highest of purposes for throwing his life away. Her eyes widened in terror and recognition. "That's Bryn, one of the last surviving humans from our village. He was one of the few humans that would talk to me after they all found out I had Bonded an Onizac. He's going to get himself killed for barging into the middle of an Onizard meeting!"

Surprisingly, the Fire Queen began to chuckle. *As long as I live? What if I kill you all before you have the chance to oppose me?*

"Death is not the end," Bryn explained, his blue eyes glaring into the Fire Queen's eyes without any sign of fear. "While we may not be able to oppose you in body forever, our spirits will live on. Surely you must know that, since when one of your kind dies a star appears in the night sky. Human beings may not have a star in their name when they die, but they do know that their spirit lives on."

The Fire Queen glared at Bryn, but it did not seem to faze the human boy. A small glimmer of triumph left her eyes as she seemed to ponder his words and what they could mean. *Very well,* she said at last, the glint coming back to her crimson eyes. *You have an opportunity to prove that theory, for you have sealed your death. You have life only until I decide to end it. But before I gain the opportunity to kill you, you shall be known as Senme. It translates to "star hope" in your tongue, and it will be a reminder to you that a human may hope for the stars, but no human can ever get above his or her station. Perhaps I can even teach you some respect before you burn alive.*

"We shall see, Fire Queen. Respect must be earned." Bryn Senme said as he walked back to the Human Leyr, running his fingers through his brown hair.

Truly odd, commented the Fire Queen. Then, as if suddenly realizing that the other Onizards were still there, she added, *All Onizards are dismissed.*

As the Onizards left for their leyrs, Jena noticed Deyraeno walking toward Rulsaesan. The Child of Light looked up to see her husband and began to sob onto his shoulder. As they embraced, Deyraeno appeared to tell her something that made her tears vanish. Rulsaesan glanced at the abandoned leyr and smiled for the briefest of moments before sobbing again.

"She knows about us, Senraeno," Jena said.

That's as it should be, Senraeno said. *I am happy that my mother is happy again.*

"But now I'm worried about Bryn, though he did the smart thing and gained the Fire Queen's curiosity. She won't kill him until she thinks she has him figured out. If anyone can confuse the Fire Queen for a long period of time, Bryn can."

Senme will be safe, Jena. We need to worry about ourselves now.

Rulsaesan and Deyraeno walked into their leyr together, their tails entwined.

My mother used to talk to me while I was still in my egg. She told me I had great potential, and that she loved me,

Senraeno explained. *Granted, she probably said that to all of my brothers and sisters as well, but it still means much to me.*

Jena nodded sadly. "It is great to have a family who loves you."

Jena, what happened to your family? Senraeno asked. *I sense great sadness from your end of our link.*

Jena sighed, and said, "It is not something you need to know right now, Senraeno. All that matters is that I have a new family now, and they love me."

What is love anyway?

"It is when you care about someone so much, you are willing to risk everything for them."

Like when you jumped off my dad's tail to rescue me?

"Exactly like that, Senraeno, though not all love is the same as the love between family members. Your mom and dad, for instance, have a different love than any sister would have for a little brother."

I don't understand, Jena.

"You will in time, Senraeno. For now, it's time for us to sleep. I can sense you're as exhausted as I am."

Good night, Jena. Senraeno said, yawning deeply. *I love you.*

"I love you too, Senraeno."

Chapter 10

Idenno watched the clouds drift toward the sea as he let his mind wander. His mood had dramatically improved from earlier in the day, though he still felt the pain from countless days of being isolated from the rest of the Sandleyr. The knowledge of the Bonded human was almost enough for him to completely ignore it, however.

We have hope again, Idenno said softly.

Indeed, came an unexpected answer from beside him. Idenno noticed Rulsaesan near the Sandleyr entrance. *We have hope kindled by the gentle heart of Idenno.*

Idenno smiled shyly before looking toward the sun slowly slipping beyond the horizon. He shifted nervously before saying, *I have done nothing, good lady. Shouldn't you be in your leyr by now? Sunset is coming, and your joinmate is waiting for you.*

I still have a few minutes before I must hide for the night, and Deyraeno knows where I am, Rulsaesan said. Her kind gray eyes glimmered, though she eyed the departing sun carefully. *Who said you have done nothing? The Fire Queen? If nothing means throwing away your own life to save mine, then protecting my hope for the future at the risk of terrible punishment, then I must wonder what happens when Idenno does something.*

Idenno smiled weakly. *I am already under the terrible punishment of the Fire Queen, but if there were any greater punishment possible, I would gladly suffer it for you, Rulsaesan, the true and future Leyrque of Day.*

Rulsaesan nodded solemnly. *I know, Iden. I will always treasure that devotion which I cannot return. Sometimes I wish I could return it, but then I look at Dey and realize everything is right in the world. It seems strange that the daylight owes her life to the rain.*

Not so strange, good lady, said Idenno, his eyes portraying a certain amount of sadness, *The rain must die for the daylight to live.*

Yet rain is never far away to bring hope to all who feel its presence, Rulsaesan said. *Nor does it die. It simply fades away for a time, until the daylight has reigned for a day. Then the rain brings a certain beauty to the world the daylight rules, and the night reigns when the moon and stars light the sky in the sunshine's place.* Rulsaesan sighed. *When I was young, I took comfort in the stars. But now I cannot; I am bound to the sun's course. I was told once that I would be a great Leyrque, but that, I'm afraid, is a dream that faded away a long time ago. You, Iden, are lucky; you can choose to walk the world at any hour, and you have more peace of mind than any Child of Light could ever have. I feel the burden of ruling constantly, Iden, even though I am not the Leyrque. I see the suffering of both humans and Onizards every day, and I can do nothing. I could not even save my own son; I am a failure.*

You are no failure, Rulsaesan, Idenno said. *You only realize you have weaknesses like the rest of us. That is the sign of a true Leyrque.* He glanced at the sun, which was nearly gone. *The sun fades away for the night to reign, and Watchzard Idenno resigns for the day.*

May the Great Lord of the Sky protect you, Idenno, Rulsaesan said.

Idenno laughed. *I shall believe in the Great Lord of the Sky again when he gets rid of the Fire Queen.*

Rulsaesan looked at the Watchzard gravely. *Do not joke about such things, Idenno. Perhaps His plan for getting rid of her is near completion as we speak.*

Chapter 11

The night was cold and quiet; mist, barely visible in the pale starlight, hung over the sleeping Sandleyr. The ruined wall of the Leyr Grounds, shrouded by darkness, no longer seemed to be a prominent mistake in the landscape. Only an Onizard with excellent vision and a great resolve could have possibly found the Watchzard rock, now abandoned in the black nightfall.

The glowing orb on his tail guided him as he limped across the ground, searching for his destination. His skin was black, and his horns were a dull gold almost indistinguishable from the rest of his body. His pale lavender eyes and the orb on his tail were the only features on his body that reflected any light. If he hid his tail from any onlookers, he would have completely blended in with his dark surroundings. But first he had to reach the Watchzard rock; it was a difficult task for him, considering his two left legs were almost completely disfigured at the shoulder and knee. It was a problem he could hide relatively well while standing, but when he limped from place to place he could not hide his pain.

Upon reaching the Watchzard rock, the black Onizard collapsed, shivering from pain and the cold. But he did not allow himself to stay on the ground for long; slowly and steadily he rose to his feet, desperately clinging onto the rock for support. There he stood unmoving for several minutes, his gaze focused on the stars above him. He noticed nothing else, not even the other Onizard in the area until she lightly touched him on the shoulder. He pulled away quickly and fearfully, though when he recognized her, he immediately regretted it.

Delsenni, he said warmly, a small smile forming as he stepped closer to her, hoping she would forgive him for his momentary lapse.

Delsenni's golden eyes gleamed in the darkness as she cautioned, *Mekanni, you should come back inside. You'll freeze to death in this weather.*

Mekanni sighed and closed his eyes. *Perhaps it would be the best thing for the Sandleyr if I froze to death.*

Don't say such things! You are the Elder Child of Light, the great Leyrkan of the Night Kingdom. The Sandleyr needs you.

Yes, I am Leyrkan; Leyrkan of a Sandleyr too afraid to speak to me. The mighty Fire Queen has clearly seen to that. More than likely, she's also cancelled the traditional meeting between Children of Light and the new Bonds. She wants to protect her son from the Night Children, after all. His grip on the Watchzard rock tightened. *I even heard an Onizard quietly muttering that you and I are not true Children of Light, claiming the Night Children only serve the darkness. I wish he were right; at least then, I would not sense their fear when I pass them, and I would not hear them calling me Mad Mekanni and other more foul names behind my back. The truth is, Delsenni, the Sandleyr would rejoice if I died tonight.*

Tears started forming in Delsenni's eyes. *If you died tonight, those who knew the truth would not rejoice.*

Yes they would, Mekanni said, looking at her with new concern. *If they did not at least pretend to rejoice, the Fire Queen would single them out and kill them slowly.*

She would have to fight them first. If she actually defeated me, then I would die slowly, and the Sandleyr would lose the last of the Night Children, Delsenni said calmly. *But first, they would both die, and Deybralfi's cruel destruction of our family would be complete.*

Mekanni's looked away from her as he began to sob. *Curse that foul fire demon for holding us all hostage! Every night I'm haunted by pain, both past and present. But as much as I want to die, I could never kill them.*

Gripping Mekanni's tail in her own, Delsenni said, *Don't let that be your only reason for living. There are other Onizards who need you.*

Really? Mekanni asked; his tone was filled with doubt. *Who could possibly need me?*

The look Delsenni gave him told the answer before she said anything. *Your joinmate, the Onizard who loves you, needs you now more than ever before.*

Worry temporarily replaced his despair as he gazed into her eyes. *I could never give up my love for you. If only I were worthy of the love of such a beautiful and noble lady.*

You are worthy if I say you are worthy. Delsenni said in a matter-of-fact tone. *Besides, I should be the one worrying about self-worth. You are still Leyrkan Mekanni, the most honorable Onizard in the Sandleyr. Nothing the Fire Queen has ever done can change that.*

Delsenni looked Mekanni directly in the eyes, and it was enough to drive away his suicidal thoughts for the moment. He knew that she loved him even through the pain that he involuntarily made her feel on a nightly basis, and he could almost believe the praise he gave her.

She seemed to wait until she was sure Mekanni was giving her his fullest attention before she added in a somewhat playful tone, *Now let's get back inside before we both freeze to death!*

Very well, my lady, Mekanni said, chuckling in spite of the pain. He gladly watched Delsenni lead the way back to the Sandleyr, but before he followed, he carefully bowed to an imagined Onizard near the Watchzard rock.

Chapter 12

Jena opened her eyes and saw sunlight streaming through the Sandleyr entrance. This was not right; the Human Leyr was on the Invitation Hall floor, and a long pathway to the main section of it made the leyr secluded from the prying eyes of Onizards. Sunlight was not visible from that area; the Fire Queen had decided that was for the best, since the daylight brought a certain amount of happiness she determined humans had no right to have. Jena sluggishly glanced about at unfamiliar surroundings and became nervous as she tried to remember what she was doing here.

When Senraeno awakened a short time later, all of her memories of the previous day returned to her.

"Well, we're already disobeying your dad's orders," Jena said sadly.

Yes, but at least we're avoiding those two scary Onizards Teltrena told us about.

"You actually believe they exist?" Jena asked incredulously.

I'd have to assume that they do. You heard what Teltrena said; she heard the Mad Mekaguy screaming herself.

"You can't always believe what you hear, Senraeno. Teltrena didn't actually see who was screaming. How does she know that the Fire Queen wasn't screaming herself?"

Because that would be extremely mean of her and not right. Senraeno replied matter-of-factly, acting insulted at the very suggestion.

"Not everyone does what is right, Senrae," Jena said sadly.

You mean the Fire Queen does what is wrong? Senraeno appeared terrified.

"That is why we are hiding up here," Jena said.

But that's awful! Poor Teltrena!

47

"Yes, poor Teltrena. Poor everyone who has had to deal with her wrath."

Now you're acting sad again, Jena, like when I asked about your family.

"That's probably because I was thinking about my mother. She is gone forever because of the Fire Queen."

You mean she went to the stars? Senraeno asked in terror.

"Yes, I'm afraid she did."

Senraeno stood in thought for a long time. *I think we should go to sleep and wait for nightfall. If the Onizards Teltrena mentioned were real, I'm sure they're really nice.*

"I suppose we'll have to wait and see, Senrae. But let's stay awake a while longer. I want to see if Teltrena can get Alair back to me."

Chapter 13

Teltrena awakened and cursed herself for not remembering to visit Delbralfi after the Sandleyr meeting. Normally she wouldn't be worried about the welfare of a human being's pet, but now that she had acted above her station by healing Senraeno, she had to consider the sacred pact of a Child of Earth. She had to be concerned for the welfare of those she healed until the day either she or the healed creature died. She still believed in the pact, even if she was a mere non-nature now, and she had to accept the responsibility that came with it. Senraeno's welfare would be compromised if his Bond was upset over a missing pet. Now she was going to need some excuse to speak to Delbralfi again that didn't make her sound like a complete and utter fool.

It surprised Teltrena that she even cared about looking like a fool anymore. By now she was almost used to the insults and shame that came with being a non-nature, to the point that one more Onizard thinking she was a useless fool should not have mattered anymore. She could not understand why she cared about the opinion of a Child of Fire she had only met yesterday, but she supposed her concern came from his previous kindness to her. She didn't want to make the one Onizard who was kind to her think she was not worthy of his kindness.

Teltrena stepped outside of her leyr and walked across the Invitation Hall. The other Onizards stepped away from her in fear as she went to the underground lake to take a drink of the cold water. Even the Child of Earth who had attacked her yesterday was avoiding her path.

Excuse me, miss, said a Child of Wind. *How did you become friends with one of the most frightening Onizards in the Sandleyr?*

I have no idea what you're talking about, the non-nature said, giving him a stern look of disapproval. *I have no friends, and I am late to my duties. Please leave me alone.*

When she went outside to gather information for her report, Idenno reacted to this story with laughter. *How could a newly Bonded Onizard possibly be frightening?*

Apparently his bloodline is what makes him frightening; I can't think of anything else they could criticize him for.

If they're frightened of him because of his bloodline, they are fools. He doesn't even look like the Fire Queen!

I know! laughed Teltrena. *He must have gotten his looks from his father.*

An awkward pause ensued as Idenno narrowed his eyes and smirked. *Maybe so, but why is Lady Non-nature eyeing his looks?*

I wasn't. I just meant to say-

Sure, make your excuses if that's what you wish, Idenno laughed. *In the meantime, I have a favor to ask that involves you paying a visit to your dear Delbralfi.*

My dear Delbralfi? Don't be silly, Idenno; I don't even know him, and I certainly don't have any desire to call anyone my dear.

Fair enough, I shall say no more, then. I suppose if you just want to leave Jena's things down there, that's fine for you. I'm just trying to help both you and her out by creating a valid excuse for you being there.

What's in it for you, and why do you know I have to go back there? Teltrena asked curiously.

Everyone knows about the Child of Earth's pact between the creatures he or she heals, Teltrena. I had to assume that his Bond's happiness is important to his welfare. As for what's in it for me, I only want a chance to meet my namesake.

Deldenno scampered about the leyr, chasing the Onizac about and giggling as only a small child can do. When he chased Alair to the entrance, he nearly ran into Teltrena as she stood outside.

Bral, the nature lady is here! he shouted as he ran toward the back of the leyr.

Delbralfi yawned and stretched his wings. *Nature lady?* he asked sleepily.

Yep, the lady who you said was a pretty Child of Earth, but she said she isn't.

When the Child of Fire noticed Teltrena, Deldenno had to laugh as his Bond suddenly straightened up and looked concerned.

Hello, Teltrena. To what do we owe your visit?

It's not dismal news this time, Teltrena said. *Watchzard Idenno only wants to meet Deldenno. A reasonable request, I suppose, considering Deldenno is named after him.*

A request I'm sure Delden would be glad to grant, Delbralfi said before turning to the Child of Water in question. *Would you like to go outside?*

Outside! Outside! Deldenno squealed excitedly. *Is it raining outside?*

No, I'm afraid not, Teltrena said, *though it is a nice day outside.*

No fair! I like the rain! Well, is Idenno nice?

Yes, he is, Teltrena said. *Though he can seem odd at times, he truly is a nice Onizard at heart.*

Well, I guess we'll go then, Bral!

Sure, Delden, he said, though as he lifted his Bond to his back he turned to Teltrena and spoke to her privately.

Delden was too excited to ask Delbralfi what he said to her for the time being. He was going outside!

I shall speak to you alone in a moment. Feel free to gather Jena's things while I am gone.

Teltrena blinked in surprise as she watched the two Bonds leave their leyr. *It shouldn't be this easy to get the girl's things from him,* she thought to herself. Why was he not grief-stricken like he was the evening before? Surely a friend should have put up a greater struggle to keep all memories of his dead friend that he could, but there wasn't even the slightest hint of a tear in his eyes as he told her to gather Jena's things.

A terrifying thought crossed Teltrena's mind as she picked up a stray piece of clothing, a thought she prayed was not the truth. What if the grief he showed yesterday was all an act? What if he wanted to see another human dead, and had arranged for this to happen from the beginning? What if he was truly like his mother, and any kindness he had shown to anyone was only an attempt to get something he wanted?

You probably shouldn't take Alair, Delbralfi said as he entered his home. *The Fire Queen thinks he belongs to me, and so did the rest of the Sandleyr, as far as I was aware.*

Teltrena tensed in fear. *Won't they know the truth when he dies in a few days from the loss of his Bond? I think he'd be better off in the care of the Children of Earth, where at least he can spend his last hours in relative peace.*

The Onizac stepped forward and stared at her, almost as if he was trying to tell Delbralfi that she was lying.

If Delbralfi noticed the Onizac's actions, he ignored them. *Present company excepted, I don't trust the Children of Earth. They tend to prolong unnecessary suffering. Besides, he makes a lot of noise. When the Fire Queen hears him, she will seek him out and find my dead friend,* the Child of Fire explained. *I don't want her loss to be felt a second time.*

You make a valid point, Teltrena admitted, thankful her previous fears were unfounded. *She-*

Delbralfi waved his tail in negation. *There's no need to tell me anything else. I don't need or want to know anything else. However, if Idenno ever wants to see Delden again, please be his messenger.*

I will do my best, Lord Delbralfi, Teltrena said, *though I am the messenger for the entire Sandleyr, not just the Watchzard.*

She bowed and took her leave, but the smile she had was killed when she stepped outside of her leyr to be greeted by the glaring eyes of the Fire Queen.

What were you doing in my son's leyr yesterday, non-nature?

D-Deyraeno said it would be a good idea to tell him his slave was dead.

Since when did you take orders from Deyraeno? she exclaimed, her mental voice burning into Teltrena's brain.

I-I don't. I just thought it seemed like a good idea, so I-

You thought? The Fire Queen laughed harshly. *I am the one who thinks, not you. You are too stupid to think properly. I warn you, if I catch you out of line again, I will make you wish you had never failed your last healing assignment. Now, what were you doing there today?*

Teltrena tensed, trying to explain why she was carrying Jena's things in her tail.

She was disposing of the slave's things, Delbralfi said as he came to her rescue once again. *I did not want to bother with it myself, so I sent for the non-nature.*

Well done, my son, the Fire Queen said, at once appearing almost relaxed. *It was wise of you to put her in her place,* she added with a glare in Teltrena's direction. *Keep a cautious eye on her, Delbralfi; she is a cursed Onizard who brings trouble to all she cares about.*

Yes, my queen, Delbralfi said, his eyes lowered to the ground. *While you are here, I was wondering about the slave boy. The one you called Senme? I would like to put him in his place.*

The last time you tried to put a human in her place, she could have Bonded, the Fire Queen growled in anger.

No, she could not have Bonded. You said yourself humans cannot Bond. I only tricked her into going to a death trap. I believe I can do the same for the Senme boy.

We shall see, the Fire Queen said. *In the meantime, non-nature, your rations are cut in half. There's no need for you to waste food.*

Yes, my queen, Teltrena said, but inwardly she shouted her anger at the Great Lord of the Sky. How was she supposed to get food to Jena and Senraeno if she was starving from her own lack of food?

Go see if the slaves can make use of the girl's things, then destroy the rest, the Fire Queen commanded.

Yes, my queen. Whatever you wish.

Chapter 14

"Somehow I don't think we'll be seeing Teltrena again today," Jena said as she watched Delbralfi bring his Bond back to their leyr.

Jena, I'm scared of the Fire Queen. What if she tries to hurt us?

"We're well protected here; if she tries to harm us, there are many Onizards who will step in the way. Besides, by the time she finds us, you'll be big and strong."

But Teltrena's big and strong, and she's still scared of the Fire Queen.

"She may be scared, but she could beat the Fire Queen if she had to fight her."

You really think so? the young Onizard appeared concerned for his friend.

"Of course. Now get some sleep before nightfall; we'll want to be awake when we meet Mekanni and Delsenni."

The outside of the Sandleyr was no longer as cold as the previous night, and the Night Children were taking advantage of the pleasant weather by stargazing together. All was happy, until Mekanni stirred and noticed something in the Sandleyr below.

There is someone awake down there, he said warily to Delsenni. *Can you sense it?*

I can, but I don't understand it, Delsenni admitted. *That leyr has been abandoned for quite some time now.*

Ten times the green plants have died and grown again since that leyr was inhabited, Mekanni commented. *No one will claim it. They know an evil Onizard inhabited it, yet they won't do anything about her now that she's Queen.*

Someone is either brave or stupid to be down there. We should pay them no heed.

Bravery for the most part is stupidity, Delsenni, Mekanni said. *No doubt they're just a couple of fools who wish to see if the rumors are true about us. I suppose you should go down there and discourage them.*

Mek, we cannot judge them like this. Perhaps we should leave whoever it is alone. They will learn over the course of the night that the rumors are lies, and we can be at peace again.

Senni, what if I become sick again? the Leyrkan of Night asked as his two left legs tensed. *I don't want to worry about others if I can't even remember who truly matters.*

Worry appeared in the Lady of Night's eyes as she surveyed her mate nervously. *You think you're going to have another attack soon?*

The warning signs are there, though I think I should be able to hold it off. It's just that I was thinking about that poor child of Rulsaesan, and-

Say no more. I will drive away all distractions, Mek. Don't worry; I will handle our guests myself.

I don't think anyone else is awake, Jena, Senraeno said sadly. *Maybe my dad said we should stay awake at night just to avoid everyone.*

Jena had to agree with Senraeno; the Sandleyr had been completely silent, and she had not seen any signs of Onizards moving about since nightfall. "If that was his intention, it was a good idea. We'll have to tell Teltrena that Mad Mekanni doesn't exist."

How very kind of you to admit that, said a female voice Jena did not recognize.

The two Bonds ran to the back of the leyr and watched the ledge, which slowly became more illuminated by the orb on the tail of the mysterious Onizard. Her skin was pure black; her only other visible features were her golden eyes and her bright saffron horns. A piece of the front horn was broken off at the tip, which, combined with her proud stance, gave her the appearance of an Onizard used to many battles. There was something strangely familiar about her, like a long-forgotten and pleasant memory. Yet there could be no doubt that this Onizard was deadly when she wished to be.

"Who are you?" the human girl asked in an attempt to hide her fear.

I am Lady Delsenni, the great and powerful Child of Light, the black Onizard answered, *but I am the one who should be*

55

asking why a young human is playing in a leyr that is not hers. How did you come up here, and why are you here?

She is here because of me, Senraeno said. *I led her here.*

Jena did not know how she should feel about his quick learning in telling half-truths. "We were brought here by Deyraeno of the Day Kingdom. He told us to seek the protection of the Night Kingdom."

Deyraeno would never tell such stories of Mad Mekanni, Delsenni said, a bitter tone entering her mental voice. *He is an old friend, and he knows how such stories could hurt my Mek. Explain your real purpose here, or I shall have to deal with you in less than pleasant ways,* she added as she held out the claws on her right foot.

"Forgive us, Lady Delsenni," Jena said. "We were only repeating a rumor we heard from a non-nature. We do not actually believe the rumors."

Delsenni glared toward the direction Jena's voice came from. *Why do you hide from me, then?*

"We cannot truly trust anyone unless we know they don't serve the Fire Queen. She will kill us if she ever finds us."

Suddenly, Delsenni lowered her foot again. She began to laugh, and her laughter filled the leyr for a long time before she said, *How could I serve the demon who destroyed my life and killed all happiness in the Night Kingdom? You do not have to fear me, child; simply show yourself. I am certain I can protect you to the best of my abilities.*

Jena cautiously stepped out of the shadows and bowed to the Child of Light. "My name is Jena, Lady Delsenni."

And I am Senraeno, her Bond, he added as he followed behind her, doing his best to bow as well.

Delsenni blinked in surprise. *Aren't you two supposed to be dead?*

"With all due respect, my lady, shouldn't you be the last Onizard to trust rumors?"

Lady Delsenni smiled. *Normally I wouldn't trust gossip, but yesternight I heard an Onizard talking about seeing Idenno wailing and extremely upset about the loss. Idenno wouldn't lie about a child of Rulsaesan; it isn't in his heart.*

"He was lying to protect us," Jena explained. "Everyone is afraid that the Fire Queen will kill us if she discovers us for what we are."

They have a good reason to be afraid, Delsenni said, a hint of sadness in her voice. *But come, children, I will take you to Mekanni. I'm sure we can both get you some food, and we'll both be glad for some company. We haven't really had a decent conversation with anyone else in years.*

Jena and Senraeno let the Lady of Night lift them onto her back, and once they were settled she took off for the entrance.

I must warn you, children, that you must avoid three subjects with Mekanni. Do not stare at his legs or ask what happened to him, do not discuss the Fire Queen, and do not ask about our lack of children in front of him, Delsenni commanded.

Why? Senraeno asked.

It was what Jena wondered as well, though she was not quite ready to risk asking.

Mekanni occasionally has bouts of sickness. Those three conversations usually are what starts it, and when he gets sick, he forgets who he is or where he is. He suffers in agony, remembering the pain he received the night we lost our hope for the future.

"Is that where the rumors of him screaming came from?" Jena asked.

Yes. Delsenni said slowly. *I ask you to avoid those topics for his protection. I love him so, and I don't want him to get sick again. I am the only one who can bring him out of it, and it's gotten harder each time.*

"Don't worry, Lady Delsenni, we won't say a word."

When they arrived outside the entrance, Jena noticed another black Onizard sitting on the Watchzard rock. He seemed taller than Delsenni until he got off the rock to meet them. Jena tried desperately not to stare at his left legs, but she could not help dwelling on them for a moment or two longer than was polite. She could not even guess how Leyrkan Mekanni had survived for so long with legs so mangled.

May I ask why you have brought our uninvited guests? Mekanni asked his mate.

I have invited them now, Mek. They are Jena and her Bond, Senraeno. They are friends of Idenno.

The Leyrkan of Night stared at Jena and Senraeno for a long time before a small smile appeared on his face. *Idenno always was good at acting. You two must be the children who were declared dead.*

We are, Senraeno said. *My dad said it was a good idea to pretend to be dead.*

Your dad is a very smart Onizard, Mekanni said. *I'm sure he's proud to have you as a son,* He paused for a moment before he smiled and added, *A human has Bonded at last. Imagine what this means, Delsenni.*

We will have to protect them until Senraeno is older. Then, when they are discovered, the demon will be frightened for the first time since I gave her that scar.

"That was you?" Jena said, in total awe.

Yes, the Lady of Night admitted. *Though that is a story for another time, when all is happy again,* she added. Her eyes darted quickly to Mekanni, making it clear to Jena that she was trying to steer the topic of conversation in a different direction. This night was getting more awkward by the second.

"Could we have something to eat before we continue our conversation?" Jena asked. "Senraeno and I haven't eaten since late in the afternoon yesterday."

Of course, children! Mekanni and I haven't eaten either, so we shall enjoy our early evening meal together. I shall be right back with some sweet grass.

Jena gasped. Sweet grass was supposedly a rare plant; the Fire Queen had forbidden humans from eating it, but Delbralfi had once stolen a piece for her. She remembered how much it resembled its description, and how disappointed she was when she realized she would never be able to eat it again.

True to her word, though, Delsenni returned with a tail full of sweet grass. *The Fire Queen thinks I don't know where she hides it all,* the Lady of Night explained, *but she has always underestimated me. Please, enjoy your food.*

Jena and Senraeno ate their share gleefully, thankful that they had gotten something to eat that was better than the standard Onizard diet of grains and sea oats that grew near the Sandleyr. Mekanni, however, did not eat the portion his mate had set on the Watchzard rock for him.

Mekanni, please eat; you're worrying me, Delsenni chided.

I'm not hungry at the moment, he replied, sounding rather harsh. Perhaps more harshly than he intended, since he glanced toward Delsenni with an apologetic look before continuing with, *I am curious about our guests. Jena, how did you manage to get Invited in the first place? That is the one thing in this situation that I do not understand.*

My Onizard friend asked me to stand on his ledge with him. It was a good thing I agreed; I don't think he would have managed it on his own. He was quite nervous.

Naturally, laughed Mekanni. *I suppose your friend would be jealous of you now if he wasn't sad about your apparent death.*

Jealous of what? Senraeno asked.

Jealous of Jena Bonding, of course, Mekanni laughed. *Though being jealous of death is always a possibility as well,* he added as he sighed.

"Well, he enjoys life, despite his status," Jena said carefully. She did not know how her new friends would react when they knew the name of her Onizard friend, but if the Fire Queen was a forbidden topic of conversation, the two would probably not be pleased to know Jena was friends with the Fire Queen's son. "He doesn't have a reason to be jealous of me, though; he Bonded as well. I saw them before all the chaos broke out on the Leyr Grounds; Deldenno seems like he'll grow up to be as kind as his Bond."

Jena was confused by the looks on faces of the two Children of Light. They did not have the look of shock that normally came when she mentioned Delbralfi to others; they seemed extremely interested in her friend.

You are friends with Delbralfi, son of the Fire Queen? Mekanni asked.

"Yes. Don't worry, though, he's nothing like his mother. He's actually helped protect me from her a few times."

Delsenni smiled. *It seems there are many strange things about you, Jena. It is fortunate that you decided to stay awake at night instead of the day. We can take over Delbralfi's job for a while and make sure you are fed well. In return, I ask that you keep us company. It gets lonely having no one to talk to, despite my love of speaking with Mekanni.*

Perhaps when Senraeno is older I can even teach him how to use his powers, Mekanni said. *I used to be a Child of Water before I gained my true form, so I'm certain I can help, if you don't mind a crippled Onizard who lost his only fight teaching you how to duel.*

I wouldn't mind at all, Leyrkan Mekanni, Senraeno said happily.

Well, since it is nearly morning, I shall take you two back to bed, Delsenni said. *You have no idea how happy we are to have you in the Night Kingdom. Thank you for ignoring the rumors about us.*

"You are welcome, Lady Delsenni. Thank you for making it easy to ignore the rumors."

Chapter 15

At dawn, Teltrena carefully removed the pile of dirt that was covering Jena's things. It had been difficult work convincing the Fire Queen that it was all destroyed, and some of the tattered clothing was rendered useless, but overall it was a sacrifice that was for the best. She also grabbed a small pile of grains before she took off for the formerly abandoned leyr.

The non-nature entered the leyr to find Senraeno resting and Jena sitting quietly in the corner. *I've brought you your things,* she said, wondering if Jena had fallen asleep in her vigil.

"Thank you, Teltrena," the human said, "You've been a wonderful friend to us."

I haven't been anyone's friend, Teltrena said. *I'm only doing my duty.*

"The duty of a Child of Earth?"

No, the duty of any decent Onizard. Did you see if the rumor was true?

"Well, Mekanni and Delsenni exist, but they weren't wrathful or evil. If anything, they seemed extremely sad. Apparently the Fire Queen's reign has hurt them greatly. Delsenni was especially vocal about her hatred of the Fire Queen."

I like her already, Teltrena said, smiling as she began to place Jena's things around the leyr. Any Onizard who was brave enough to be vocal about their dislike of the Fire Queen instantly earned her respect.

"She's very pretty and brave; she said she was the one who gave the Fire Queen that scar."

Teltrena froze. *She was? Are you sure she wasn't lying?*

"Yes, I'm completely certain. Who would lie about something like that?"

Certainly not me, the non-nature sighed. *Well, I suppose that they have a way to get you food? That was my main worry; the Fire Queen will catch me if I take more than my fair share.*

They do, though it involves theft from the Fire Queen.

Well, you can have this to help out, Teltrena said, depositing her food onto the ground. *It isn't much, but it should be enough to feed a human and a growing hatchling for a meal or two.*

"Thank you, Teltrena," the girl said. "Despite what you say, you have been our friend."

Well, I'd better leave before someone suspects something, Teltrena said, taking off in order to avoid an argument on that subject.

She wasn't anyone's friend. Friends didn't fear for their own safety when they helped others, and friends didn't hide secrets from each other. Being someone's friend didn't mean getting him or her hurt due to the very act of friendship. As long as she was a non-nature, Teltrena could not be anyone's friend.

Teltrena hoped the subject of Delsenni didn't come up again. She had enough problems with her own guilt about the past; she did not want to hear or think about the Onizard who had indirectly made her a non-nature.

Chapter 16

Bryn walked cautiously toward Delbralfi's leyr. He heard the mental voices of a few Onizards speaking about the fool Senme who dared to insult the Fire Queen, but he paid them no mind. He was far more worried about what Delbralfi would do to him than about a joke name that would probably fade away over time.

The Fire Queen had said her son was harsh with renegade humans, and rumors spoke of him as a silent but strong and dangerous Onizard. Delbralfi had Bonded, of course, but that was no indication of kindness. The previous Onizard who gave him orders had been a Child of Earth, supposedly the kindest of all Onizards, but she had been cruel and unforgiving to Bryn. It was a wonder he was still living out of all of the people of his former village.

Bryn tried not to let his thoughts dwell on Jena, but he could not forget the great injustice she had suffered. She had been a kind and cheerful girl despite their situation, and he had greatly admired her for that. But now she was dead as a result of her kindness, and his bitterness towards all Onizards grew deeper. Rumor had it that Delbralfi had been the one to bring her to the place where she drowned; if this was true, he would do everything in his power to torment the Onizard before the Fire Queen killed him.

When Bryn reached the leyr of Delbralfi, the Child of Fire himself stepped out to greet him. He calmly ushered Bryn into the leyr, and once they were all inside, he seemed to relax, even smiling at the human as he said, *Welcome, Bryn.*

"Call me Senme; the rest of your kind already does."

The Onizard seemed puzzled. *Very well, Senme. As you may have been told, my name is Delbralfi.*

I'm Deldenno, his Bond! added a young Child of Water as he stepped forward. *I'm sure we could become great friends.*

"I'm even more sure we can't," the human said flatly. Bryn was disgusted with the very idea of befriending the treacherous and cruel creatures responsible for so many human deaths. He noted with a small amount of satisfaction that he had displeased his new masters.

Only time can tell on that, Delbralfi said. *In the meantime, you have no chores in this leyr, other than pretending to be working when the Fire Queen comes here. Don't worry, she doesn't come here often.*

"No chores?" Bryn blinked in surprise. First they were daring to suggest they would befriend him, and now the Child of Fire was saying something that practically made a human closer to his equal. There had to be a catch to this situation. "You're just trying to trick me into being lazy so you can turn me into your mother."

Apparently Jena never told you that I have no mother, Delbralfi sighed; if he was acting, it was certainly convincing.

"I suppose now you're going to say you were Jena's greatest friend," Bryn said. "I won't believe you; I know that she is dead because of you."

Deldenno and Delbralfi looked toward the back of the leyr, then at each other.

"There, your ruse is discovered. Jena was never your friend; you only said that to make me trust you into giving away something important. Jena was far too smart to have an Onizard for a friend."

That is enough, Delbralfi said as he lowered his head closer to Bryn. His eyes were narrowed in a glare that sent shivers up Bryn's spine. *Do you know how much her loss has tortured me? No, I suppose not. All Onizards are just the same, and all children are exactly like their parents. I'm a sadistic monster who only lives to kill. Go ahead and believe that if you want; I do not care if you judge me, for I know who I truly am. I can take insults to my character, but I will not take insults to hers for trusting me!*

Bryn stood in shocked silence.

There is a way to prove my story. You remember what made Jena unique from the other humans?

"Her cheerfulness," Bryn couldn't understand why Jena had been so cheerful; everyone else was always depressed. But her cheerfulness had brought happiness for a small amount of time among the humans. It had given them all hope, and now her cheerfulness was one of the many things he missed about her now that she was gone. He missed her so much, it was difficult to think about.

I would hope that wasn't unique to Jena. I was speaking of her Onizac. You are aware that Onizacs only trust creatures their Bond trust?

"Yes, of course," Bryn had many a scar from Onizac scratches.

Come here, Alair, Delbralfi said, and the Onizac emerged from the back of the leyr.

Bryn watched in amazement as Delbralfi carefully lifted Jena's Onizac and rocked him. "Jena really was your friend, wasn't she?"

Yes, one of my very few friends. She will be missed.

"Well, then I suppose you are trustworthy enough for an Onizard."

Delbralfi smirked as he let Alair go back to where he had originally been hiding. *Then I will have to suppose you are sensible enough for a human.*

"Are you calling humans insensible?" he asked, harshness returning to his voice.

Only as much as all Onizards are untrustworthy. You really should learn not to generalize, Bryn. I was joking.

"You're not allowed to joke with me, Onizard. You may have been Jena's friend, but you are not mine. You'd have to do something completely drastic to prove you're not scum like the rest of your kind."

Delbralfi shook his head. *Very well, Senme. As I said before, time will tell.*

Chapter 17

As time passed, Senraeno and Jena grew stronger under the care of the Leyrkan and Lady of Night. Though he was nowhere near his adult size, the Child of Water was no longer the small hatchling that Jena had to rescue from the floodwaters. He was now big enough to carry Jena all by himself, though he was not capable of flying yet.

One night, roughly four months after Senraeno's birth and supposed death, Mekanni surveyed him carefully before declaring, *It is time, my children.*

Time for what, my Leyrkan? Senraeno asked in his confusion.

It's time for you to begin training. Don't take my appearance as a sign I'm a loser; in a fair fight, I could have won.

Don't dwell on it, dear, Delsenni cautioned.

I know, Delsenni, Mekanni said as if his mate was being a nuisance at the moment. *I was only explaining it to him.*

I would be honored to have you train me, Senraeno said, disrupting a potential argument between the mates. *Could you teach me how to fly?*

The Leyrkan smiled. *I will certainly try. Follow me,* he said as he walked toward the area behind the Leyr Grounds.

As Jena and Senraeno followed him, they discovered that there was a path hidden there. It did not appear to be a path that was meant to be hidden, though the underbrush was starting to grow across it. Whatever the path was meant for originally, it had not been used in some time.

With no children, no one has remembered to take care of the training grounds, Delsenni explained as they all began to walk down the path. *When you are no longer in hiding, you should ask Delbralfi and Deldenno to take care of this problem with plants covering the path.*

The journey took quite some time, since Mekanni had chosen to walk with the Bonds instead of flying them there. They walked down the path with Delsenni guarding them from behind and Mekanni leading them. This continued for a short while until the trees suddenly became scarce and they found themselves on a long stretch of flat land. Parts of it were covered with short grass, but most of it was soft sand. The only landmark was a hill to their right; it was large enough for all of them to stand on and survey the surrounding area, and it was to this hill that Mekanni lead them.

The view from the top of the hill was amazing, even by Senraeno's mediocre standard of night vision. He could see his birthplace in the distance in small but breathtaking detail, and he could see the forest that stretched toward the mountains for some time. He only wished that he could see from this spot during the day and better appreciate the view.

Here we are. A perfect place to learn how to fly, Mekanni said after reaching the top of the hill. He sat down, breathing heavily from exhaustion.

Mek, are you okay? Delsenni asked.

I'm perfectly fine, Senni, he said curtly, glaring at the ground. *Your first task will be to learn how to glide, Senraeno. This place has been used for many generations of Onizards without injuries, so you don't need to worry about messing up. Don't try to do anything rash. All you need to do is get a good running start from this hill and open your wings.*

I'll try, the Child of Water said, taking a long moment to eye the area ahead of him before following Mekanni's instructions.

It was by no means the longest flight ever remembered by Onizards, but for a few brief moments Senraeno felt the wind beneath his wings and soared across the land. Admittedly, his landing was not the greatest either, but there was pride in his heart as he turned back to see the reactions of the others.

Fantastic, Senraeno! You'll be excellent at flying in no time! said the Lady of Night.

"You did a great job, Senrae," Jena said as ran up to him and hugged him.

It was a decent flight. Why don't you try again?

Mekanni's voice was completely monotone, as if he were speaking to an inanimate object instead of his friend. It was a tone he usually only reserved for when he was upset with someone, and now it made Senraeno's first attempt at flight seem utterly pitiful.

Senraeno was shocked, but he did his best to hide it. *Of course, sir.*

This same process continued throughout the night. Every time Senraeno flew, the others would praise him while Mekanni found some new flaw in his flying ability and asked him to start all over again. The whole process was completely frustrating; several of the flights that were particularly excellent by Senraeno's standards caused Mekanni to claw through the sand in frustration.

I think it's enough for one night, Delsenni said after a while. *We should go now before Senraeno becomes exhausted from all this work.*

Yes, I suppose we should head back, Mekanni agreed, though his words came slowly. *There is much work ahead of us, Senraeno, but it was a decent start.*

Thank you, sir, Senraeno said. He was much too tired to worry about the lack of conviction from Mekanni.

I can carry you if you'd like, Delsenni said to him privately.

No, my lady, I'd not like that, Senraeno sighed. *I think this is one path I have to take on my own.*

Very well, Senraeno. You did wonderfully tonight.

He knew he hadn't, but he was not going to disagree with her.

"When you're through with your training, Mekanni will be proud of you," Jena said.

I hope so, Jena. I am going to work hard to make sure I am not a disappointment to anyone.

Chapter 18

Teltrena, she is the daughter of the last Leyrque. You do not have to fear healing her.

Heal me, Teltrena! There was something inherently terrifying about those eyes, even without the terrible wound underneath one of them.

I can't! My powers...they aren't working!

You pathetic excuse for an Onizard! You are nothing but a non-nature!

Deybralfi, please. She is still just a child. She is not used to healing in public.

If she cannot heal her Fire Queen, she cannot heal anyone. She is a non-nature, and all will treat her as one as long as I rule this Sandleyr.

Teltrena awoke from her nightmare, sobbing in pain from the memory of her past. It seemed her dreams had become more frequent since the day she had healed Senraeno, and they were becoming more and more vivid as time went on. If she had a particularly nice day, for instance if she had talked to Delbralfi instead of his mother, the dreams were about happy memories instead of painful memories, but those days did not happen very often. Teltrena simply had to deal with the dreams as she dealt with everything else in her life.

Teltrena tensed as she saw the form of a Child of Fire outside her leyr. *What do you wish, my queen?*

I'd hope I'm not your queen, Delbralfi laughed as he stepped closer, revealing his face.

Teltrena smiled and shook her head. *I'm sorry. I thought you were someone else.*

Obviously, Delbralfi said with a slight shrug.

Shouldn't you be concerned about her finding you here?

It's only sunrise. The Fire Queen is always asleep at this time, and even if she was planning to suddenly change her habits, I have an excuse. I've come to ask you to take extra care in destroying this necklace. With his tail he held up a small chain made of what appeared to be silver. *It belonged to the dead girl, and I had trouble recovering it until now.*

How hard could it be to get this thing? Teltrena asked as she took it from him, trying to will herself not to blush as her tail accidentally touched his. She held it carefully, for she knew that when Delbralfi said to destroy it, he really meant to protect it even more carefully until she could give it to Jena.

My Onizac would not let me have it until now, he said.

So I see, Teltrena said as she smirked. *They can be pains sometimes.*

Yes, indeed. Delbralfi paused and looked at her carefully. *You seemed to be sad when I came here. Are you well?*

I just had a stupid dream, Teltrena sighed. *You don't need to know the details.*

You've been having dreams too? What was this one about?

I told you, she said. *You don't need to know the details.*

Tel, I'm your friend. I'm worried about you. Would it help if I told you about the nightmare I had last night?

Sure, if you want to tell a non-nature about it.

You ought to know by now that you are not a non-nature by my standards.

Teltrena felt guilty when she saw the hurt in his eyes. *I'm sorry. It's just a force of habit. What was your dream about?*

Two Onizard women were fighting one another over me.

Teltrena laughed. *That sounds like it would be pleasant.*

Delbralfi paused for a moment before he realized what she was talking about. *Not like that, Teltrena!* He exclaimed, and for a moment Teltrena thought she saw a hint more of the color red in his skin. *If that was what they were fighting over, I don't think I'd be sharing my dream with you. They were fighting to the death over whether I would live or die, and it appeared that the Onizard who wanted me to die was getting an early lead. The Onizard who wanted me to live was crying to the Great Lord of the Sky and all of the stars for help, but they were silent, and it seemed that she was slowly giving in to despair. I woke up before I knew who won.*

That does sound terrible! Teltrena said, looking at him carefully. *Since you shared your nightmare with me, it's only fair* that I share mine. My dream was about when I became a non-nature. I was trying to heal the Fire Queen, but I couldn't concentrate on the wound. I could only see how terrifying those eyes of hers were, and I failed. I could feel my mother's disappointment in me all over again. Every time I think I'm over that pain, the dream returns again to haunt me. I just want to get over it; I want to be free and happy again. But I can't help but feel that everything is my fault. I deserve to be a non-nature.

Your dream was far worse than mine, Delbralfi admitted. *It is said, though, that Children of Earth cannot heal the wound of an evil Onizard. It wasn't your fault, Teltrena.*

Perhaps not, but I still feel guilty about it, Teltrena sighed. *You know, this is strange. I've never talked to anyone about that before. I've always been taught that it's proper to hide emotions, but with you...it seems right to share them.*

Delbralfi smiled. *Well, you can talk to me if you need a friend to discuss things with.*

As long as the Fire Queen doesn't see you talking to me.

Forget my mother! If I suffer for a short while what you have suffered for all this time, so be it.

Though I'm grateful for your concern, I don't want you and Deldenno to suffer on my account.

Nevertheless, you are welcome to talk to me any time. I'll leave for the time being; the Fire Queen will be awake soon.

Good-bye, Delbralfi, Teltrena said as she watched him leave. When he was gone, she turned around and sighed. What was going on? She should not be wishing that he could stay longer when she knew it would cause him pain and suffering at the claws of his own mother.

It was dawn, though, and the non-nature had errands to run. Thoughts of Delbralfi could be put off for another dream.

Chapter 19

Bryn stood up and rubbed the last tears of a nightmare from his eyes. Now that he had stood up to the Fire Queen without any show of cowardice, it didn't make sense to let others see the fears he truly felt. He had to at least put off his death for a while, even if he hadn't figured out his reason for continuing to live yet.

"Jena," he said, a whisper not meant to be heard by anyone living. She had shown such resolve in the years after her mother's death, even though he knew she had to be grieving with all her heart. He had to wonder now what had kept her so strong all those years, especially since they had both been mere children when it happened. Was it the same motivation that drove him now to be stoic and unafraid? Did she, too, fear an emotional collapse if her true feelings gave way?

He tried to force himself to stop thinking about her and how she must have died afraid and alone. How he wished he had been there to help her, to show her she had a friend she could count on!

Bryn refused to let himself think about what he had wanted to tell her, for it was too late to dwell on such things. It was his secret, and if she could never know, then neither would anyone else.

"Time to play Senme," he sighed as he rose out of his uncomfortable stone bed and began to prepare for another day as the Fire Prince's slave.

Chapter 20

Teltrena watched the Watchzard dancing with Deldenno and laughed. *I worried something like this would happen; you're corrupting him.*

Perhaps, Idenno said to her privately. *But it seems you have the power of corruption as well, since his Bond trusted you with that necklace.*

Don't start that again, Idenno. Delbralfi is only a friend. I'm the only one who can sneak in and out of that leyr without notice. He knew I was the only logical choice of Onizard to bring the necklace.

If you say so, the Watchzard snickered.

What do you think that thing is for, Teltrena? Deldenno asked. *It doesn't seem too important to me, but Bral wouldn't even let me hold it.*

It doesn't matter what it's for; it's not ours, so we cannot use it, she said. *Hopefully I'll be able to get it to Jena quickly before I inform the Fire Queen that the Watchzard is still dismal.*

The young Child of Water sighed. *Why do you have to lie like that, Teltrena?*

If she doesn't, you won't be able to talk to me anymore, Delden, the Watchzard explained.

Well, I guess it's a good thing she's nice enough to lie for us, Deldenno said.

Teltrena smiled. *I'm happy to lie for you, Deldenno. Since I can't legally heal anymore, I want to help others in anyway that I can.*

By doing something that loses the respect of other Onizards? You certainly have changed in these last few months, Idenno said.

For the better, I hope.

Indeed. You're actually almost fun to talk to now, Idenno said with a wink.

73

Thank you. The sentiment is mutual.

There was a time when you guys weren't fun to talk to? Deldenno asked, seeming as if he were in shock.

Sure, Idenno said. *I was depressed because I thought I was becoming useless, Lady Non-nature was depressed because she thought being a Child of Earth was the most important thing she could aspire to-*

I still think being a Child of Earth is important, Teltrena interrupted. *Their powers help many Onizards who would otherwise walk around with permanent injuries.*

Yes, but you don't go around thinking that following a strict set of rules for helping others makes you a good and kind Onizard.

Teltrena nodded in defeat, unwilling to get into an argument with Idenno over something so petty. *True. The point is, we were both different Onizards, but we have changed for the better.*

Delden! called Delbralfi as he emerged from the Sandleyr entrance. *Oh. Hello, Teltrena.*

Hi, Delbralfi, Teltrena said. *I am going to destroy the necklace before I report to the Fire Queen. She is still sleeping, so all is safe.*

That is good to hear. Delden, I fear it is time for us to leave for now. Watchzard Idenno is busy now.

I'm hardly busy, Idenno shrugged. *Few Onizards ever come up here anyway, and Deldenno is good company.*

I'm sure Teltrena needs her time to speak to you to gather information for the report, though. I don't want to delay her any further; she doesn't have enough time as it is.

True, Idenno said. *Well, visit any time you'd like, Delden.*

See you soon, Iden! The younger Child of Water said before the two flew into the Sandleyr entrance again. Admittedly, Deldenno's flight was far more awkward than his Bond's flight, but he was still able to fly inside on his own.

Idenno turned to Teltrena and smirked. *It seems your dear Delbralfi is concerned about you.*

He's not my dear, she said quickly.

I'll bet you're his dear, though, Idenno managed to say as he laughed merrily.

Teltrena frowned as utter frustration took over her thoughts. *I should ask Rulsaesan who your dear is, just so I can tease you as much as you tease me for this silly nonsense you claim to be true.*

Idenno's laughter ceased immediately. *That's no secret; I'm surprised you don't know, since even the Fire Queen knows.*

What, you actually do have a dear? Teltrena blinked a few times to be certain she had heard correctly. She did not expect such a response from Idenno, who wasn't exactly the most social of the Onizards.

Well, she's my dear, but I'm not her dear, so to speak, Idenno stared at the ground and kicked at the sand, as if it was his last desperate attempt to avoid the non-nature's gaze. *So I must be content to be her protector.*

Teltrena took a few moments to think. *It actually is Rulsaesan, isn't it?*

The silence from the Watchzard confirmed her guess.

Idenno, she is a joinmated Onizard; it's just not proper for you to have those feelings for her. You need to get over her.

Easy for you to say, Lady Non-nature; you have never actually been in love, Idenno said, raising his head slowly. *When you fall in love, you will understand. I have no desire to take away the complete happiness she has with Deyraeno; I am the one who told her to tell him how she felt about him. When you truly love someone, you only want to see him or her happy; though it hurts deeply if they do not love you in return, you would rather die than take away their happiness. I would die to protect Deyraeno, because I am his friend, and because he makes Rulsaesan happy. I would die to protect her, because I love her. If standing on this Watchzard rock for the rest of my life was all that it took to make her and her family live in complete bliss for the rest of their lives, I would proudly stand on this Watchzard rock for the rest of my life. So I find myself here talking to you.*

You'd be miserable for the rest of your life out of love? Teltrena shook her head. *That's not fair to you.*

Love is not about the Onizard who loves, Teltrena; love is about the Onizard who is loved. So Rulsaesan is happy with Deyraeno, and she appreciates what she cannot return.

Teltrena frowned as she said, *But a part of you dies every day you stand up here alone.*

Idenno smiled. *But Rulsaesan is alive and well, and that makes me happy when all other happiness dies.*

Teltrena sighed. *I do not understand what you are trying to tell me.*

I hope you will someday. Love is a beautiful thing, even if it is unreturned. Life is worth living just knowing that it exists.

If you say so, Watchzard Idenno, Teltrena said as she pondered how to end the awkward turn the conversation had taken. *I am going to give the necklace to Jena now.*

Remember what I said when you actually do find a dear, Teltrena.

If I ever find a dear.

You will, Idenno said with firm conviction in his tone.

Teltrena flew back into the Sandleyr, doubting Idenno's last statement, and pondering his strange logic.

Chapter 21

Jena, are you awake?

As she recognized the mental voice of Teltrena, the human girl stood up slowly, rubbing her eyes. *What is it? Senraeno and I are exhausted.* It had been a long night of flight lessons, but Jena was determined to keep that a secret. Though it seemed the non-nature was on their side, she was still the Fire Queen's messenger. To survive long in that position, someone had to be very good at deception.

You've been asleep all day. I've been trying to wake you up, but you obviously couldn't hear me. Teltrena scolded. *I nearly lost this.* She added, holding up a small shiny object.

Jena blinked in confusion. Shiny objects didn't normally exist in the Sandleyr, and the ones that did were not usually considered something worthy of giving a non-nature to be shown to a human. In a confused state, Jena walked over to see the object and gasped in shock and sudden pain renewed. "My mother's necklace! Delbralfi thinks I'm ready to have it now?"

He told me that your Onizac was guarding it.

"He was lying to you. As much as I love Alair, neither of us would trust him with something this important," Jena gazed for a long time at the simple silver chain. "Why does he think I'm ready for it now?"

You have accomplished many things since you Bonded Senraeno; staying hidden here for this long is an accomplishment on its own. Though I don't understand why his opinion on your readiness to have it would matter. It belongs to you, does it not?

Jena sat down on the dirt floor, her eyes focused on the necklace. "I was very young when my mother died, and this necklace is the only tangible thing that proves she ever existed. It's very important to me; I made him promise to protect it for me until he thought I was responsible enough to have it."

Well, if my opinion matters at all, I think you are ready for it, and obviously he does too.

"He must trust you a great deal, Teltrena. He was even reluctant to let Rulsaesan see it when she asked about it."

Teltrena shook her head. *I doubt it, if he lied about your Onizac like that.*

"But he gave you the necklace, and that makes you very trustworthy in my eyes. He was probably only lying because I made him promise not to tell anyone about our agreement."

Perhaps. I do not know Delbralfi's thoughts.

As Teltrena got lost in some thought of her own, Jena grinned as an idea occurred to her. "He'd probably tell you, if you asked him."

Jena, that is highly improper. His thoughts are his own, as my duties are my own.

"Fair enough," Jena looked at the necklace again and carefully fastened it around her neck before saying, "Thank you, Teltrena. This means much to me."

It looks good on you, Jena.

The human sighed. "It looked better on my mother, but thank you."

After an awkward moment of silence, Teltrena said, *Well, I must be going now. It is nearly dusk.*

"Good-bye, Teltrena," Jena said as the non-nature exited the leyr. After Teltrena left, Jena's thoughts stayed focused on the necklace until her Bond awakened a few minutes later.

Jena, where did that come from? Senraeno asked, pointing to the necklace with his tail.

"A memory. But come, Mekanni will be waiting for us soon," Jena did her best to hide the emotional stress she felt, for she knew that the subject of her mother would only make the training that night even more difficult.

Chapter 22

Senraeno, you must concentrate! Mekanni shouted. *How do you expect to defeat the Fire Queen if you cannot even lift yourself off the ground?*

Senraeno sighed. Mekanni was asking him to carry Jena across the field while attempting to destroy a stone target at the end of the field. He had gotten better at flying and carrying Jena, but he just couldn't muster up the energy to fire a blast of water at the target. He suspected that he hadn't gained the ability yet.

Mekanni, he is trying his best, Delsenni said softly, as if she did not expect him to listen.

Trying is not good enough for me. Trying to survive will only get him killed, or worse.

I'm getting better, at least, Senraeno said hopefully.

Getting better? Mekanni cringed as he put too much weight on his mangled legs in an attempt to stand up straighter. *Do you have any idea whatsoever of what you're up against? The Fire Queen will not fight fair, and she will watch you for your weaknesses. She will delight in finding out what makes you scream in terror, and once she finds out, you had better pray to the Lord of the Sky that she kills you quickly. But she will not kill you quickly.*

Jena, you will be the lucky one; the Fire Queen will more than likely simply roast you with her breath of flames and watch you scream in pain as you die a slow and incredibly painful death. She will wait to do that, however, until she is finished with Senraeno, and she will hurt Senraeno in ways he would have not thought possible.

The Leyrkan of Night trembled as he spoke to them, and there was a harsh reality in his speech that could only come from one who had seen many dark things.

Senraeno sensed the Leyrkan's words had caused Jena a great amount of emotional pain. It was not the normal pain of sympathy for their teacher and friend; something Mekanni had said had truly hurt her. Jena would not let Senraeno see what was happening in her head, but he could tell his Bond was hiding a terrible secret from them all. After a few moments of silence, she burst into tears and ran toward the path to the Sandleyr.

Jena! You are needed here! Mekanni shouted in a frustrated tone.

Mekanni, stop at once! Delsenni screamed. *You are making yourself physically sick, and your speech is not helping them.*

They deserve to know the truth! I am telling them something far more valuable than platitudes about how wonderful they are for failing.

They are children, Mek! Don't punish them for what she did to you.

I am not punishing them! he explained as he seemed to struggle maintaining his stern glare. *I am only trying to warn them so that they don't end up like me, a useless cripple.*

The three Onizards stood silently for a few agonizing moments. Delsenni tried to wrap her tail around Mekanni, but he simply pushed her away.

I will talk to the girl, she said coldly as she backed away from him. *If it makes you feel useful, put fear into Senraeno's heart by telling him more than he needs to know. The Child of Light I know and love would never have done this; you are stressing yourself out so much, you are not yourself. You are killing your spirit, Mek, and it scares me.*

My spirit died a long time ago, Senni, he said. *The sickness took it away for good.*

No, it did not. Your own pathetic attitude is what is making you this way. You criticize Senraeno for not trying, and yet you won't even try to fight for yourself.

Mekanni turned away from her. *Talk to the girl, then. Don't blame me when things go wrong and they are helpless, just like the others were. Just like I was, and still am.*

After a long moment, Delsenni said, *You are not a useless cripple, Mekanni. What happened in the past was not your fault. I only wish I could make you see the Onizard I see in you.*

She turned and walked away, disappearing into the forest. Only Senraeno saw Mekanni's silent tears.

Jena sat on the wall overlooking the sea, turning her back on the world in general. Mekanni had been far too harsh on Senraeno in those last few weeks, and that night was the worst of all. She shivered in fear as she recalled the Leyrkan's description of a human death from the Fire Queen, and she privately wondered where he had obtained such knowledge.

The girl did not even notice Delsenni until the Lady of Night gently touched her on the shoulder. *Jena, are you okay?*

"I've had better nights."

We all have, Delsenni admitted. *Please don't blame Mekanni for his actions. Ever since our only egg failed to hatch, he has been obsessed with preventing further suffering in the Sandleyr. As much as I don't condone his behavior tonight, in some ways I'm rather glad he's found you two to care about; it keeps him from worrying about being sick again, and it brings joy to his heart when you do well. I hope that doesn't make me selfish.*

"You're not selfish, Delsenni," Jena shrugged. "I was foolish to run away from the truth like that."

You were upset, Jena, and you still are. Under the circumstances, you were perfectly justified. I only wish I knew what was bothering you so much.

Jena sighed deeply and looked at the Lady of Night in the eyes. She had very rarely seen the kind of concern Delsenni had shown to her, and the secret that she kept inside her heart was starting to become too much of a burden to handle. Not even Senraeno knew the full truth, and that was a difficult thing to keep from a Bond.

"The Fire Queen burned my mother to death."

If she was shocked, Delsenni hid her shock by gently hugging Jena with her tail. There was something peaceful and almost motherly about it that would have made Jena smile in any other situation. *I am so sorry, dear. If Mekanni had known, he would not have said those things.*

"He doesn't really need to know; it's one of those things I don't like thinking about. Delbralfi is the only other being who knows the full story, and that is only because he was there when I found out," Jena breathed deeply, trying to avoid another bout of crying as she began to tell Delsenni her story.

"The Fire Queen did not even notice my mother and I until six summers ago, when I Bonded Alair. It was a complete accident; I was just walking to my next chore when a baby

Onizac started following me. It was then that I suddenly became a threat in the Fire Queen's eyes.

"I was only ten when it happened, so I had no clue what kind of danger I was in. Delbralfi kept me busy by telling me to play hide in the shadows, and I thought it was all just a silly game.

"But after a week of this, Alair was missing one morning. I looked all over Delbralfi's leyr, but he was nowhere to be seen. Just when Delbralfi and I feared the worst, Alair returned. But he was carrying my mother's necklace.

"My mother never took that necklace off, so I became fearful. Then, I heard a long, terrible scream that went on for some time before it was finally silenced. In my heart, I knew that my mother somehow was punished because of me.

"Delbralfi and I cried on each other's shoulders that day. I suppose he had lost his mother at the same time I had."

"He explained later why his mother was fearful of an Onizac Bonded to a human, but I always shrugged it off; it's not easy thinking that my mother died because of me," she added, glancing toward the Sandleyr entrance.

Your mother knew her sacrifice was not in vain, Delsenni comforted. *I am certain that she wanted the best life for you that you could possibly have, even if it meant leaving you. She would be proud of the young woman you have become.*

"Do you really think so?"

You are a wonderful human being who was brave enough to risk your life for a hatchling of the same species as the foul creature who killed your mother. That is not what many can say.

Jena shrugged and wiped away a few stray tears. "That was nothing, Lady Delsenni. I knew that the Fire Queen was nothing like the other Onizards. Besides, how do you know my mom would be proud of me?"

All mothers are proud of their children, Jena. I would have been very proud of my child if I had gotten the chance to know him or her. Someday, if you become a mother, you will be proud of your children. It is just the way mothers are.

"The Fire Queen isn't proud of Delbralfi. She hates him."

Delsenni smiled sadly. *She is not a true mother to him then, is she?* The Child of Light wrapped her tail around Jena comfortingly. *Your strength, courage, and determination would make any mother proud. Your mother is watching from the stars and smiling at the wonderful daughter she has.*

"You think so?"

I know so. Now wipe away those tears and trust in yourself like I trust in you.

"I only hope that I can do the best I can to prove my worth. I think that's what my mother would have wanted."

You've proven your worth to me, Jena. Now all you can do is prove it to the Sandleyr, As she glanced toward the forest, she added, *I think it is time we went back and talked to Mekanni. If I know him, he's worried sick about us and terrified that he's made me leave him forever. What a silly idea.*

"You don't mean Mekanni's version of sick, do you?"

No, Delsenni said, *Though we should be getting back anyway. I'm starting to become worried sick about him.*

Senraeno watched Mekanni in fear. The elder Onizard had not spoken since Delsenni had left, and he had not stopped crying either. It was becoming more and more clear to the Child of Water that Delsenni was what kept Mekanni sane. She had been gone for some time, and if she did not return soon, Senraeno did not know if he could help Mekanni avoid the sickness.

Leyrkan, are you okay?

I will be fine, Dey, as long as you stop calling me Leyrkan. Delsenfi will return soon, and I will finally be able to prove my love to her in front of all the Night Kingdom, Mekanni said. *I am glad you are here with me to make sure I don't get too nervous to propose.*

Senraeno could see that the Leyrkan's eyes were not focused on anything in particular, and it frightened him. *Leyrkan, I don't know who Delsenfi is, but I know Delsenni will be coming back in no time.*

Deyraeno, you ought to know who Delsenfi is. You were there when we first met. Speaking of which, how are things going between you and Rulsaena? You'd better tell her how you feel about her before my brother does.

The Child of Water blinked a few times in an attempt to sort out this strange information. *I'm Senraeno, sir. I think you're starting to get sick.*

Nonsense, Deyraeno. I'm fine. Delsenfi and Idenno will be here soon. What are you nervous about?

Leyrkan Mekanni, I am not Deyraeno. I am his son. You're starting to scare me.

83

Mekanni shook his head and blinked several times before taking a long look at Senraeno. *You are Senraeno. I am so sorry.*

Are you okay?

I'm perfectly fine, he said as he avoided Senraeno's gaze. *Where is Lady Delsenni?*

I'm here, said the Lady of Night as she stepped out of the forest with Jena.

Senni! Mekanni exclaimed as he made his way to her as quickly as he could. *I am so sorry, Senni. You were right; all of this frustration is making me ill.*

I'm sorry too, Mek; I should not have been harsh on you, and I most certainly should not have left you.

Senni, you can't be with me all of the time, and you should not try to defend me all of the time either. The Leyrkan said with a grim smile. *I was being too harsh on Senraeno; I just wanted him to know how to protect himself, and I had forgotten that he is still just a child.*

I think it is time we all just forgave each other and moved on with our lives, Senraeno said.

Everyone agreed as they laughed nervously.

Well, let's get back to the Sandleyr before sunrise, said Mekanni. As they began to walk back, he added, *Thank you, Senraeno, for saving me.*

For what?

I would have descended further into sickness again if you had not been there to talk some sense into me.

Well, it's only repayment for you saving me.

Now when did I save you?

When you decided to teach me how to use my abilities, despite my inability to control them.

Mekanni smiled. *You are welcome, Senraeno. You have been a good pupil. I'm proud of you.*

Senraeno stopped you from becoming sick? Delsenni asked after the two Bonds had gone to sleep.

He did. I barely understand it myself. So far you have been the only Onizard who has been able to control it somewhat, and that is mostly because you are my mate and can pass for your former self, Mekanni said. *Then again, his mother is the Lady of Day, so it is possible he has the blood of Light within him. It traveled along my family line for as long as the Sandleyr existed; perhaps it's time for a new bloodline to begin.*

That makes no sense, Mek. You and I are perfectly healthy, or at least a close equivalent to perfectly healthy, and Senraeno isn't showing any signs of illness from staying awake at night.

There has been no Day Child for some time. The Sandleyr needs one. Why not Senraeno?

Senraeno was not even considered a possibility when Ammasan died. She could not have named a nonexistent child her heir!

When did I ever say he was Ammasan's heir? Mekanni said curtly.

Delsenni's eyes widened in sudden horror. *You don't think that Rulsaesan is-*

We have to consider the possibilities, Senni. She has lasted ten years without the aid of another Child of Light to share the burdens of the Sandleyr's emotions. That alone is an accomplishment that will rank her among the great Leyrques of the past. But even the mightiest of Leyrques cannot survive that amount of pain forever.

She has Deyraeno as her mate and your brother as Watchzard, Delsenni said. *Their love could keep her alive until their bodies could not stay in this world any longer. Besides, the new Child of Day will come soon, and we will not have to give up Senraeno to the Day Kingdom. I know it.*

Mekanni nodded. *As much as I want him to succeed, I don't want Senraeno to become Senraesan. He is a good Onizard, a child I wish was my true son. Besides, it's selfish of me to start thinking about others as potential Day Children. I want someone to restore order to the Day Kingdom and drive away the Fire Queen for good, but it is not right to wish that burden on others.*

Delsenni sighed. *He's still only a child. A child cannot become a Child of Light anyway, so we shouldn't be having this discussion.*

You are right. I suppose, as usual, that I am just trying to rationalize something that cannot be explained.

After a long moment of silence, Delsenni said, *Let's go to bed, it's nearly morning.*

Mekanni sighed. *May the sun set on a better Sandleyr.*

Let Rulsaesan rule the day, and let Mekanni continue to rule the night.

Chapter 23

Rulsaesan awakened early and walked over to her ledge to watch the other inhabitants of the Sandleyr start their days. She noted the human called Senme walking slowly toward Delbralfi's leyr and waved her tail to him. He ignored this gesture of friendship, however, and scowled in her direction.

Rulsaesan sighed. It was not her fault that Ammasan had not chosen an heir to receive her powers when she died. It was not her fault that Ammasan's daughter had used an ancient loophole in Sandleyr law to gain her power. The suffering Rulsaesan felt each day as she watched the other inhabitants of the Sandleyr go about their business was enough to make her sick if she was not careful, but she could do nothing about it. She could not claim the title of Leyrque until she had another Child of Light as her apprentice, and Ammasan was staying silent for the time being.

Rulsaesan felt especially sorry for Delbralfi. Before he was even hatched, he had been used as a pawn for the Fire Queen to gain power. Under Sandleyr law, if no Child of Light had gained their powers after the death of a Leyrque or Leyrkan, the eldest descendant of the former Child of Light who had children was designated temporary King or Queen until the new Child of Light was found. It was a ridiculous rule that rarely needed to be enforced in the past; the new Child of Light was never missing for ten whole years, like had happened in this case. The suffering in the Sandleyr was great, and neither Rulsaesan nor Delbralfi could do anything about it.

Rulsaesan knew, though, that a new Child of Light would gain his or her powers soon. She wouldn't be able to explain it to anyone, not even Deyraeno, but she knew in her heart the time for the new Child of Light was coming. The thought made her smile, but it also brought a sense of worry to her. The most likely candidate in Rulsaesan's eyes was Delbralfi, and he was not protected well from the terrifying eyes of the Fire Queen.

Rulsaesan shuddered at the thought of those eyes. Before she became a Child of Light, she would not have noticed anything unusual about the Fire Queen's eyes; they were a normal shade of red, after all. But Rulsaesan's power of empathy grew stronger as she looked into an Onizard's eyes, and what she felt when she looked into the Fire Queen's eyes was nothing but heartless anger and cold hatred. Rulsaesan was glad she had Deyraeno to protect her from those eyes.

Rulsaesan glanced back at her sleeping joinmate and smiled. She felt extremely lucky to have the devotion and love he showed her every day, and she always tried her best to show him the same love he gave her. Sometimes she feared her love was not enough for such a good Onizard; after all, he had received attention from other young ladies in his youth. She knew, though, that he would never consider another Onizard, and that gave her the happiness that kept her alive despite feeling the pain of the suffering around her. Deyraeno might never believe her when she told him his love kept her alive, but she knew in her heart that it was the truth.

Rulsaesan saw her son Deldenno running outside of his leyr to greet Senme before he flew toward the Sandleyr entrance, and smiled at the thought of how much he was like his namesake. Idenno had been a good friend to both her and Deyraeno, even to the point of confronting the Fire Queen to protect them. He had sacrificed his standing in the Sandleyr for them, and had given up all hope of ever seeing his own family again. Rulsaesan felt guilty about this, for she knew that Idenno was so devoted because he loved her. But she could never return that love, despite Idenno's worthiness for an Onizard who loved him in return. She could not leave the perfection she had with Deyraeno, and she was shocked that Idenno had accepted that harsh fact so gently. Rulsaesan truly was the luckiest Onizard alive to have the love of the two greatest Onizards in the Sandleyr.

The Lady of Day glanced up toward the abandoned leyr, shifting her thoughts to Jena and the necklace. Rulsaesan extended her powers as best as she could and found that her son's Bond was distraught. Frowning, she did not notice that Deyraeno had awakened until he spoke to her.

What are you thinking about?

Rulsaesan sighed. *Jena will need to know the whole story about her mother's death if she ever hopes to confront the Fire Queen with a clean conscience.*

Surely she should know what happened by now, Deyraeno said, walking next to her.

Rulsaesan could not help smiling as she felt his love as she felt him next to her at the same time. *I doubt that Delbralfi ever told her everything I explained to him that day. She was always too young to know or understand, and I always cautioned him not to tell her. I was selfish, Dey.*

That's not selfish, my love; you were only trying to protect her.

I was trying to protect myself from the pain. I did not want to feel her pain as I dealt with my own guilt. But I am strong enough to tell her now.

You will jeopardize them by going up there. Don't think the Fire Queen will not be watching you.

She will not be watching me when she is sleeping, Rulsaesan said. *I'm not stupid or unaware of the danger of speaking to Jena, but I can use my powers to discover when the Fire Queen is sleeping, and I will tell Jena then.*

Don't overextend yourself, Rulsae. You are not Leyrque yet, and I worry about you.

I know, Dey, Rulsaesan knew quite well how much he worried, and she loved him for it. *I am not as fragile as light, though. It is time Jena knew the full truth. When she knows, both she and Senraeno will be stronger for it.*

I hope you are right.

I know I am right. I only need to preserve my strength until I am ready to tell her. In the meantime, let us stay here and wait for good things to start happening in the Sandleyr.

Chapter 24

"I meant it when I told you, Child of Fire, that I will never trust an Onizard. Please stop trying to be friends with me; it won't do you any good."

Delbralfi sighed. No matter how hard he tried, he could not get through to Bryn. *It won't do you any good to try to persuade me to stop trying, Senme. It's just not like me to give up on someone.*

"Yet you claim to have given up on the Fire Queen."

That is different, Delbralfi said softly. *I was never attached to her to begin with. She abandoned me pretty much after I was born. Rulsaesan was the Onizard who acted like the mother I never had. I imagine that is one of the reasons why she did not have children of her own for so long.*

"Poor abandoned Fire Prince," the human said as he rolled his eyes.

I am not asking for sympathy from anyone; I am only stating the truth.

"Yet you use it as an excuse to try to sympathize with me; it won't work, because deep down, you're simply a spoiled Fire Prince. Jena's mother was heartlessly murdered by the creature you casually brush off your connections with, as if the Fire Queen were nothing more than a mere nuisance to you. But deep down, you fear her greatly, because your actions do not reflect the ill-chosen words you say to me. Not once have you ever actually stood up and confronted the Fire Queen for what she is; you're too timid."

That's right, I am afraid, Delbralfi admitted. *But not for myself. If I had ever actually stood up to her, the Fire Queen would kill those I care about. I stayed silent all those years, because I knew if I said anything, the Fire Queen would kill Jena just as she killed Jena's mother.*

"You protected her? I heard you led Jena to her death."

You heard a lie.

"Is it? You were the one that had her stand with you during the Invitation ceremony. If you had not brought her with you, she would still be alive right now."

Do not blame me for Jena's decision to go, Delbralfi said, his anger rising. *I only asked her to stand with me because I thought, if she Bonded, it would prove to the other Onizards that we are equals.*

"Prove that we are equals?" Bryn Senme scowled at the Child of Fire. "So a slave has to join the hierarchy of the slave masters to somehow trick everyone into thinking they are equal."

No, that is not what I meant. I-

"Don't talk to me, Fire Prince. I'm only here to clean your floor for you."

Delbralfi sighed. *Even now, I risk the safety of myself and my Bond in order to keep the Fire Queen from killing you. Does that mean nothing to you?*

"Why keep me alive? Everyone I had to live for is dead. My only hope now is to join them in the stars, or wherever the humans go when they die."

You are the only human being in this Sandleyr who still carries their memory. If you die, no one will remember their names, or even care that they existed. Do you really want the Fire Queen's lies to be the only thing left of your family and friends?

"No," Senme said softly. "But I am not a worthy keeper of her memory."

After a moment's pause, the Child of Fire said, *No one is, but people like Jena will live on in the stories we tell each passing generation. They will be greater than even the stars.*

"Why?"

Because, in spite of living in a world that did not care about them, they still took the time to care about others. That is what matters the most.

Bryn started to smile, until he glanced toward the leyr entrance and froze in fear. Delbralfi looked up and noticed Teltrena standing there smiling at them both.

"She will betray us to the Fire Queen!" the human shouted.

Nonsense, Delbralfi said, annoyed at the very suggestion. He was halfway tempted to admit what he knew about Jena's presumed death, but common sense told him to stay silent on that subject.

I am on your side, Bryn called Senme, she added as she stepped in.

"Sure, I'm supposed to believe the Fire Queen's messenger and the Fire Prince."

If I am the Fire Queen's messenger, I suppose you are the Fire Queen's errand boy, Teltrena said. *My position in the Sandleyr does not define who I am. I do not work for her by choice, and I am doing the best I can to fight against her.*

"By doing what, talking to the Fire Prince and a human? It sounds like you're the most rebellious Onizard in the Sandleyr."

No, by protecting those who need her help, Delbralfi said. He could take insults to himself, but there was something about the way the human talked about Teltrena that made him angry.

"Now what is that supposed to mean?"

It means that there are things more important than the knowledge of angry individuals, Teltrena said curtly.

This silenced Bryn for long enough to let Delbralfi change the topic of conversation. *So, what brings you here, Teltrena?*

It wasn't important. I can see you are busy; I'll just go now.

You don't have to go now, if you don't want to leave.

Teltrena hesitated. *Well, it was a private subject. I can simply speak to you later.*

Okay, Delbralfi said, doing his best to hide the sadness he felt. *Hopefully I'll see you soon.*

As soon as I am able to come again. Until then, good-bye.

After Teltrena left, Delbralfi caught Bryn laughing. *What is so funny?*

"This is too precious; the Fire Prince and the Queen's messenger, joined in a conspiracy of passion."

What? Delbralfi blinked several times in shock. *You have it all wrong. Teltrena is just a friend of mine.*

"Good luck convincing everyone else that. I don't even know you or care about your personal life, and I noticed."

You didn't notice anything. Even if you had, I--well, it would not work out.

"Why not? You're the Fire Prince; you can have whoever you want in the Sandleyr."

First of all, I am not the Fire Prince; that implies I'm inheriting the Fire Queen's rule after she is gone, and I will not. I refuse, because Rulsaesan is the true ruler of this Sandleyr. Secondly, I cannot have whomever I want in the Sandleyr, because the Fire Queen would see her as a threat to her rule and make certain that her spirit was killed. If I had feelings for anyone in this Sandleyr, she would never know. I refuse to let anyone get hurt on my account.

"Fair enough. Pretend you're protecting her. Just don't wait until she's dead before you tell her. You'll regret it," Bryn said before picking up his cleaning supplies and exiting the leyr as if he had something far more important to do.

Delbralfi watched him leave and became lost in his thoughts, pondering the anger of Senme from a new perspective.

Chapter 25

Jena paced about the leyr as she tried to will herself into sleeping for a few hours before nightfall. She was worried about facing Mekanni again after the horrible night they had all experienced. She knew the Leyrkan had forgiven her, and she knew that everyone would pretend that things were well again. But from what Senraeno had told her, it seemed that it was Jena's fault that Mekanni had started getting sick again, and she could not forgive herself for that.

"So many have suffered for me," she said to herself as her hand strayed almost involuntarily to the necklace. First her mother suffered for her, now Mekanni and Delsenni. How long would it be before someone else lost their life or their sanity? Delbralfi had not warned her about the great responsibility that would come from being a Bond, but she knew there was no way he could have known. This terrible guilt was something Jena had to deal with on her own.

But you do not need to suffer for them.

Jena glanced toward the ledge in shock, remembering the mental voice as the voice of Rulsaesan.

The Lady of Day raised her tail to her mouth, as if asking for silence. *Do not worry. As long as Delsenni does not decide to plague the Fire Queen with nightmares, we are safe.*

"Delsenni can do that?" Jena asked incredulously.

Of course. Even when she sleeps, Delsenni has more power over her surroundings than you realize. But I shall say no more on that subject, for it is a secret only Children of Light are supposed to know.

"I understand. Why have you come, Lady Rulsaesan?" Jena asked as she curtsied.

There's no need for formalities, Jena. I am not Leyrque yet, and you are my son's Bond. In a way, that makes you a sort of adopted daughter to me.

"I don't know if you'd want me as a daughter, though; I caused my own mother's death."

That nonsense is not what Deyma would have wanted you to believe.

Jena blinked in surprise, then cautiously looked Rulsaesan in the eyes. "How do you know my mother's name?"

Because your mother was one of my best friends, Rulsaesan explained.

Jena stood speechless; her mother had mentioned an Onizard friend occasionally, but she had always assumed that Onizard was someone less important than the last Child of Light to dwell in the Day Kingdom. But she believed Rulsaesan; her mother rarely gave her name to anyone, and had instructed Jena to be equally cautious with her name. If Rulsaesan knew her mother's name, it was obvious that her mother trusted Rulsaesan a great deal.

Rulsaesan slowly continued by saying, *I do not know what Delbralfi told you about the day she died, but I hope that he did not imply that it was your fault in any way. Deyma did not want that to happen.*

Jena sighed and braced herself. "What happened the day my mother went to the stars?"

The Fire Queen, as you may know, was searching for the human who Bonded an Onizac. A description of a human with dark red hair was going about the gossip circles, and the gossip circles are usually filled with the cruelest of the Onizards. They would not have hesitated in betraying you to the Fire Queen.

"That's why Delbralfi told me to hide in the shadows. I was still quite young; I just thought it was a game he had invented."

He didn't want you to be afraid. None of us did. Your mother couldn't speak to you in those last days, for I insisted that she should stay hidden as well, for she had the same hair color as you, and I feared that she would be mistaken for you.

"That is what happened in the end, though. It's my fault."

No, it is not, Jena. If it is anyone's fault, it is mine.

"Why?"

My reasoning for protecting her was what gave her the idea that led to her death. Rulsaesan paused for a moment as she glanced away from Jena, as if trying to hide her pain. *Perhaps it would be better if you see the memory for yourself.*

"How is that possible?"

Rulsaesan held up her tail and touched Jena on the head. Suddenly, Jena was in a completely different time and place.

Deyma was tired and showing signs of aging before her time. Rulsaesan could tell she was deeply worried, and even scared, but since Deyma's eyes were turned away from the Lady of Day, she could not tell what was wrong with her friend. Rulsaesan could see a baby Onizac squirming in Deyma's arm, and she became greatly worried herself.

What is wrong, my friend?

The human woman looked up, her eyes full of tears. "I was just waiting until you awakened before I said good-bye."

Rulsaesan suddenly noticed that Deyma had taken off her necklace. *Deyma, where is the gift your husband gave to you?*

"With Alair. He will take it to Jena once his job is done."

What job? Deyma, what are you planning?

"You said yourself that the Fire Queen wouldn't be able to tell the difference between me and Jena. I am going to take advantage of that so Jena can be safe."

You'll get yourself killed! There has to be a better way than this.

"Please don't argue with me; you'll make it harder than it needs to be," Deyma turned away from Rulsaesan and looked across the Invitation Hall. "If I don't do this now, that demon will not rest until she finds the human who Bonded the Onizac. But if she sees me holding an Onizac that is clearly not mine, and I explain that the Bonding rumor was only my attempt at covering my theft, she will leave Jena in peace.

"You don't have a child yet, Rulsaesan, but when you do you'll realize I have no choice in this matter."

I understand, Deyma, though I don't like this path, the memory vision suddenly became blurry as Rulsaesan of the past began to cry. *I had hoped there would be a better way.*

"As did I," Deyma said.

Remember me when you go to the stars.

"I could never forget you, Rulsaesan," Jena's mother said as she hugged Rulsaesan's leg. "Please watch out for Jena for me."

I will. Delbralfi will take care of her too.

Deyma began to walk out of the leyr before she paused, turned around, and said, "If what they say about Onizacs is true, I hope Jena Bonds one of your children."

It would be the greatest of honors.

After she was certain the memory was over, Jena began to sob. "I never knew she chose to replace me. I always thought she was just unlucky enough to cross the Fire Queen when Alair was around."

I told Delbralfi not to tell you, Rulsaesan explained. *I didn't know how you would react, and I was upset that I had not done anything to save her.*

"You shouldn't be upset, Rulsaesan. My mother was stubborn; she would not have let you save her, even if you had tried. Your support probably meant a great deal more to her than any of us could realize."

You forgive me, then, for not telling you before?

"There is nothing to forgive, Rulsaesan. In the same situation, I would have probably done the same thing."

Rulsaesan smiled. *Well, at least all of her wishes came true. Deyma is probably manipulating events from the stars. She and Ammasan are laughing at us right now, knowing how this story will end.*

"Maybe so, but Ammasan at least is probably just glad she has a good Onizard who took her place as Leyrque."

Not yet. Ammasan must first be glad that she has a good Onizard to be the next Child of Light. But I know Deyma is proud of her daughter.

"Thank you, Rulsaesan," Jena said as she hugged her. "That means a lot to me."

Chapter 26

Senraeno awakened to what sounded like an argument coming from the Invitation Hall. Jena was still sleeping, apparently exhausted after the previous night. The sound of arguing Onizards worried the Child of Water, though; after Delsenni and Mekanni's argument, he did not want to deal with any more such stresses. Why couldn't they just keep training in peace?

Senraeno, stay hidden in the shadows and do not speak, even to me. Carry Jena there as well, if she is sleeping out in the open.

Senraeno blinked in surprise and fear. Delsenni's tone was more serious than usual, as if they had something worse to fear than her mate's sickness.

You're saying you have no clue where it went? shouted an Onizard Senraeno barely recognized.

I would not want to touch anything that belonged to you, Mekanni said. He sounded as if he was trying to pretend he was perfectly calm, but his mental voice was shaking too much.

Quickly, Senraeno carried Jena to the shadows and hid, listening carefully to the conversation.

Really, Leyrkan of Night? That is rather amusing, coming from you.

Silence, fire demon! Mekanni shouted.

You expect me to listen to a washed-up Onizard who can't even keep his legs straight? The Fire Queen cackled. It had to be the Fire Queen, if Mekanni was calling her such things. *You're so pathetic; I could knock you over before you even tried to attack me. The worst thing you can do is start screaming about the past, and no one will listen to you.*

The Sandleyr has more ears than you think, and not every Onizard is afraid of you.

But the ones who matter are afraid of me. I can tell you still fear me a great deal, and it amuses me greatly.

Back away, demon, and leave the Night Kingdom alone! Mekanni shrieked.

Now you speak more empty threats, and they do nothing to frighten me away. They actually amuse me even more, though I usually prefer other ways of amusing myself.

Step away from him, or you will have to deal with me, Delsenni's voice joined the conversation for the first time.

Delsenni, there seemed to be a sense of fear in the Fire Queen's voice. Senraeno assumed Delsenni had been hiding in the shadows until this point. *What an unpleasant surprise.*

That's Lady Delsenni to you, demon. The feeling is mutual.

Blame whoever stole the sweet grass. I had been saving it for my son's birthday, and now it's all gone and the celebration is ruined. Whoever stole it shall pay dearly.

I highly doubt you would save anything for your son, for any reason. Neither Mekanni nor I saw anyone stealing it, so leave us in peace.

How would you know? You have no child, as far as I recall. It's a pity that Mekanni could not give you the child you so desired.

Silence, demon. Delsenni's mental voice trembled like a volcano holding back its explosion. *That had nothing to do with Mekanni, and you know it.*

Really? From what I heard, if Mekanni hadn't injured himself, you could have had a child. Then again, you couldn't even produce a healthy egg, so perhaps it is your fault.

It had nothing to do with Mekanni, Delsenni said, her tone more firm and angry than Senraeno had ever heard it before.

If you say so, Lady of Night. Make sure you watch to make certain no renegades try to steal any more sweet grass. In the meantime, I shall simply have to pay my son a visit without the sweet grass.

I'm sure he'd be thrilled. Delsenni said in a deadpan tone.

More thrilled than you will be, if I discover you knew something about the disappearance of the sweet grass.

I assure you, neither of us saw anyone taking it. The Night Kingdom is deserted.

As it should be, with two mad rulers running it.

Senraeno heard loud stomping coming from below, and hoped that it was the Fire Queen leaving. He did not like hearing that conversation; he could not understand what they were talking about, but it seemed the Fire Queen was delighting in making his mentors upset.

Mad rulers indeed, scoffed Delsenni. *Mad at her, definitely, but not mad. Mekanni?*

Delsenfi, she was going to get me.

No she was not, Mekanni. Delsenfi was here to protect you.

You'll always protect me from the eyes, right Delsenfi? You won't leave?

Of course, Mekanni. I think it is time we both rested for a while.

Lead the way, Delsenfi. I love you.

I love you, too, my Mek, the Lady of Night said softly, with only the slightest hint of sadness in her tone.

Senraeno heard them walking away, and said privately to Delsenni, *I assume practice is cancelled for the evening.*

Yes! But do not worry, Senraeno; his sickness will pass. He's just had a rough night; it's tough battling both the sickness and his archenemy at the same time. He will get better now that she is gone. Just get some rest, and you will see Mekanni again tomorrow night.

Senraeno tried to obey Delsenni's orders, but he found that he could not sleep. He was too afraid for Mekanni, and for whoever would get the blame for the sweet grass theft.

Chapter 27

    Teltrena walked carefully toward the Fire Queen's leyr, anxious to get the meeting over with. She had heard screaming from that portion of the Sandleyr earlier in the morning, and she hoped she would not find some scene of carnage awaiting her. There was also the Fire Queen's temper to consider; if she was in a murdering mood, there was no way Teltrena would be able to see Delbralfi that day, and she wanted to know why he had not simply told her the truth about the necklace.
    Teltrena could not understand why it bothered her, but she felt hurt that he did not trust her with the truth. She had, after all, trusted him with her darkest secret. When she thought he had trusted her, it was refreshing to believe that there might actually be an Onizard who was honest with her. But Teltrena knew in her heart that it was too good to be true; no one could trust a non-nature, not even Delbralfi. It was a joke to think he even cared about why she had become a non-nature; she was a useless being, and she needed to remember that as she approached the Fire Queen's leyr.
    The Fire Queen glared at her when she arrived. This was nothing new, but this time the she did not stop glaring after a few moments to tell of a new assignment. It was not the bored glare of a superior Onizard inspecting a nuisance non-nature, either. The glare seemed almost accusatory, and Teltrena had to wonder if the Fire Queen had discovered her friendship with Delbralfi.
    Where is my sweet grass, non-nature?
    Your what, my queen?
    You know exactly what; my collection of sweet grass has slowly been depleted over the last months, and I am not the one eating it.
    My queen, I did not know sweet grass even existed in the Sandleyr anymore, Teltrena said in utter confusion. If sweet

grass truly did exist, the Fire Queen had every reason to be paranoid, for the only sane Onizard who would steal from the Fire Queen had to be more powerful than her. Was there a mad Onizard roaming the Sandleyr, or would the Fire Queen soon be defeated by a more powerful challenger?

It does not exist anymore; a terrible thief stole it from me, and now I will not be able to celebrate the anniversary of the beginning of my reign.

That truly is a tragedy, my queen, Teltrena lied.

It is a tragedy, young fool, for whoever stole it has spoiled my mood, and they shall face my wrath when I find them.

Are you sure it was not simply some hungry Onizac that took it? Teltrena said in desperation.

I think not; the Onizacs fear me for some reason, and they would not venture so far from their Bonds or caverns. The theft has obviously taken place over several months, for I would have noticed if that amount of sweet grass had disappeared in just a few nights.

Well, I have no idea who took it, my queen. No one I know of would be so foolish.

Keep your eyes and ears open, non-nature. If they were foolish enough to steal from me, they will probably be even dumber than you. Perhaps you'll even be promoted to Child of Earth if you find them.

Very well, my queen, Teltrena said, though she knew she would not search for the thief or tell the Fire Queen if she found him or her. After careful thought, she had her suspicions, but she could not blame disappearing food on the dead. Besides, the Fire Queen was lying about the promotion; she needed Teltrena for news about the outside world, since she stayed secluded in her leyr all of the time. She could not afford to lose her non-nature messenger.

Also, speak to the Children of Earth to see if any of them have a cure for frequent nightmares and headaches.

Teltrena stared at the Fire Queen in complete confusion. There was definitely something wrong with her head, if she was admitting such weaknesses to Teltrena. *I'm no Child of Earth, but I'm certain there is no cure for bad dreams except more sleep.*

Wonderful, mumbled the Fire Queen. *Talk to them anyway. They'll obviously know more than a foolish non-nature.*

As you wish, my queen, Teltrena said as she left, quickly seeking the first Child of Earth she could find in order to say she had actually sought out advice for the Fire Queen. Walking along the Invitation Hall, she saw an adult Child of Earth talking to a Child of Wind who appeared to be around Deldenno and Senraeno's age. Teltrena assumed he was their brother. He was shorter and thinner than his brothers, but that was typical of Children of Wind. Their jobs relied on speed, not power. Given the way he was flying in circles around the Child of Earth, he appeared to be nearly ready to become a full Child of Wind.

Excuse me, Teltrena said as she walked cautiously toward them. *Are you two Bonds?*

Yes, we are, said the Child of Earth. Her mental voice was light and friendly. *My name is Ransenna, and this is Delculble.*

My name is Teltrena the non-nature. I'm glad to meet you both.

A pleasure to meet you, too, said Delculble. He smiled a little too enthusiastically, as if he was trying to show that he was ignoring that Teltrena was a non-nature. *What brings you to us, miss?*

The Fire Queen wanted to know if there was a cure for frequent nightmares and headaches, Teltrena rolled her eyes. *She won't listen to me, even though I was a Child of Earth at one point.*

A cure for frequent nightmares and headaches? Ransenna laughed. *The only cure for nightmares is to resolve the issues that caused them. So, the Fire Queen finally got a conscience, eh?*

I suppose so, if that is what is causing the nightmares.

Well, in the case of the Fire Queen, even if there was a cure, I would never tell it to that terrible demon. It's about time she got a conscience, and she deserves nightmares, for what she has done.

I'm not sure of what you speak.

The mistreatment of the poor human beings, of course, said Ransenna. *Though frankly, I feel sorry for you too, for having to be her messenger.*

It's not too bad, if you don't incite her temper, Teltrena said. *It's rather unusual to meet an Onizard who doesn't like the treatment of humans, though.*

Well, I used to believe those lies she told us all about how humans were useless creatures with no hearts or emotions, creatures who would not care about others, even as they were dying. Sometimes I was crueler to them then I needed to be, because I thought they had no souls. Ransenna shuddered, as if recalling something terrible. *Then I was Invited, only to have my Bond nearly drown before I could save him. But then, the strangest thing happened; a human girl rescued him, without any thought of her own safety. Now she is dead, and Delculble and I still live. It bothers me a great deal, especially to hear the Fire Queen's talk of her as something horrid.*

That girl certainly was something, Teltrena said. It seemed Jena found a new way to surprise her almost every time she heard about her from someone else.

Indeed. It certainly is a pity you never met her; if you don't already respect the humans, I'd bet you would after you met her.

I bet I would, Teltrena said as she resisted the urge to smile. *Well, thank you for your help, Ransenna. It was nice meeting you both.*

You are welcome, Teltrena. Good luck, and feel free to talk to us any time.

Thank you, Ransenna and Delculble. I appreciate it.

As Teltrena walked away, she could not help but wonder just how great Jena's influence truly was. It seemed that most Onizards she talked to remembered her fondly, even if they did not know her name. It was not enough influence to confront the Fire Queen's lies directly, but it was enough to give hope to those who needed it. Perhaps directly confronting the Fire Queen wasn't the solution after all, and people like Jena could destroy the hatred of the world with quiet kindness.

Teltrena dismissed such musings, though, as she returned to the Fire Queen's leyr. She now had to create a new half-truth to protect Ransenna and Delculble from unnecessary trouble.

The Child of Earth I talked to said that the only way to stop the nightmares is to resolve the issues that caused them. Once you do that, the headaches will go away as well.

I feared that, the Fire Queen said. *But the nightmares are only a nuisance; I can deal with them on my own.*

As you wish, my queen. Is there anything else you need me for?

No. Get out of my sight immediately.

Teltrena gladly obeyed that order, thankful to be free of the Fire Queen for a while. Now she could go back to her own thoughts without fear of retribution, and she could smirk at the Fire Queen's nightmare problem. She would not tell anyone else about it, but the situation was enough to make Teltrena laugh. The most feared Onizard of the Sandleyr was afraid of nightmares! Teltrena knew how to cure them, of course, but she would stay silent like Ransenna.

Teltrena's own nightmares had ceased as she talked to Delbralfi about her past, and she had come to terms with her mother's rejection. It was likely that the Fire Queen was just as threatening to Teltrena's mother as she was to Teltrena; after all, her mother had stayed practically secluded from the rest of the Sandleyr after Teltrena had been named a non-nature. Whatever the case had been, it was in the past, and the nightmares did not plague Teltrena anymore. Her only worries were in the present and how she would survive to see the return of prosperity to the Sandleyr.

Chapter 28

Delbralfi casually waited outside of his leyr. He had seen Teltrena conversing with two Onizards earlier, and he knew that she would soon come to talk to him. He was curious about what she wanted to speak to him about, but he could not show that curiousity to anyone else. If word got back to the Fire Queen that he was frequently having conversations with her messenger, she would not be pleasant to deal with.

"What is on your mind, Fire Prince?" Bryn asked as he stepped out of the leyr. There was not quite as much anger in the way he said the hated nickname; it was almost as if he were joking.

Why would you want to know, Senme? I thought you weren't my friend? Delbralfi said in a tone that he hoped sounded as joking as he meant it.

"I'm not, but I'd really like to know if you're planning on roasted Bryn anytime soon."

No, I'm not, Delbralfi began to laugh. *I'm just waiting for a friend.*

"Ah, you're waiting for the non-nature."

I'm waiting for Teltrena. When she arrives, you may leave.

"The great conspiracy of passion!" Bryn said, laughing as he danced with an invisible partner. "Just don't Invite me when you end up having twelve children!"

Keep it down! There might be others listening.

"You cannot keep down the flaming fires of love," Bryn said just as enthusiastically, though his voice was slightly lower in volume than before.

Flaming fires of love? You really need to get a stronger vocabulary, Senme.

"Ah, I'm just a stupid human. What do I need a vocabulary for?"

For certain, he needs common sense, Teltrena said as she made her presence known.

Delbralfi froze in fear. He had been paying attention to Bryn for the entire conversation, and had no idea when she had arrived. What had she heard, and what was she thinking about him now?

"I shall leave you two alone, then," Bryn said as he winked suggestively before running off.

What was he talking about, Delbralfi? Teltrena asked as she smiled at him.

Delbralfi grinned through his embarrassment. *A rumor he was threatening to start among the humans.*

That would explain why you both were laughing, Teltrena said.

It wouldn't explain why you wanted to speak to me alone, though.

It wouldn't? Teltrena said, grinning as she walked into the leyr.

Delbralfi grimaced. She had obviously heard a great deal, thanks to Senme and his mouth. At least she was being kind about it.

I just wanted to know why you held Jena's necklace for so long, Teltrena said. *It seems to me that she proved her readiness long ago. Random Onizards I've only just met were talking about what a great human she was.*

Well, I just wasn't certain, and after she died, well...

Yes?

I couldn't just give it to you with the rest of her things; I wasn't quite ready to trust you as completely as I trust you now.

Teltrena looked up in surprise, then smiled. *Why did you tell me that the Onizac was holding it, then?*

You wish for the truth?

Yes, of course.

Delbralfi paused hesitantly before saying, *I thought you'd think I was being silly, and that's not what I wanted.*

Silly? That's not silly. If I had lost all trace of my friend except for one thing, I would want to hold onto it for a while as well, Teltrena said before she started yawning.

That's good news, then, Delbralfi said, smiling in relief. *Well, it should be sundown by now, so perhaps you should leave before more rumors about us surface. I would not want to damage your reputation.*

I would not want to damage yours either, Teltrena said as she walked outside. She appeared to be getting ready to fly, but after a few moments of yawning she simply collapsed on the ledge.

Delbralfi bolted to the ledge, but she immediately dismissed him.

I'm fine, I'm fine. I'm just exhausted. Don't worry about me, Teltrena said as she closed her eyes and collapsed again.

Unfortunately, Deldenno chose this moment to arrive.

Bral, what happened?

Delbralfi sighed. *She just fell asleep.* He tried to nudge her awake again, but this did no good. *Bryn is never going to let me hear the end of this, but I will have to take her back to her leyr.*

Deldenno began giggling madly. *Bral and Teltrena in a leyr alone holding tails.*

Bral is not going to be alone long enough for anything like that. If word of this gets out--oh stars, I just promised her I'd protect her reputation.

I know, I know. Everyone's in their leyrs hiding from Mad Mekanni and Delsenni anyway. Except Iden; he says they're nice, but he's not allowed to talk to them.

Just don't say anything about it, Delbralfi said as he carefully lifted Teltrena onto his back. *Let's just hope I don't end up killing myself or her trying to carry her like this.*

Delbralfi took flight and soared across the Invitation Hall as best as he could with the dead weight of Teltrena on his back. He would have been angry at her if she had suddenly shown she was still awake, but she was sleeping soundly. *She must have had an extremely long day,* he said to himself. As he thought about it, he reminded himself that the Fire Queen really did work Teltrena too hard, and this was just the result of several long days. Teltrena was probably nearly sick from exhaustion, and Delbralfi realized that, despite the inconvenience, he was glad to help her.

He reached her leyr and set Teltrena gently on the ground. At the ledge, he paused to watch her sleeping, and smiled to himself. Then he came to his senses and flew back to his own leyr. Bryn was definitely never going to let him hear the end of it.

Chapter 29

Senni, there appears to be a Child of Fire carrying a Child of Earth to a leyr.

Mekanni's mate laughed at what was surely a baffled expression. *Well, stranger things have happened, I suppose. They probably wouldn't want us to know what is going on.*

I guess you're right. The Leyrkan said. *Are you ready for your training, Senraeno and Jena?*

If you are ready to teach us, Mekanni, Senraeno said. *Are you recovered from last night?*

Mekanni sighed. The boy was probably wondering what that conversation was really about, but he could not tell Senraeno the truth. He knew that would truly make him sick again, and Delsenni was already stressed enough. He did not want to forget her again.

I am fine, Senraeno. Let's go to the training grounds.

The group set out, and Mekanni walked slowly by Delsenni's side. He could see that she was greatly concerned about something, so he asked, *What is wrong, Senni?*

You know someday they'll have to know the truth, Mekanni. We cannot protect them from our sickness forever.

It is my sickness, not yours, Mekanni said, hiding his eyes from her.

I am your joinmate, Mek, and I love you. If you have a sickness, it is mine too.

Mekanni nodded slowly. *I suppose you are right. Why do the children have to know, though? I think we are right in protecting them from the truth.*

When you are sick, you say things that you shouldn't. It would be better if they hear it from us when we are both calm and of sound mind.

It would not be right to tell them so soon after a sickness attack, though, Mekanni said.

There is always a threat of sickness, Mek. We cannot put it off forever.

Why are you so desperate to speak of that night, Senni?

The Lady of Night stood still for a moment before saying, *There are some truths that I want to be known so that I can put it behind me.*

I don't want to know where you were during the time I lost my memory, Senni. I don't want to know why you abandoned me when I needed you, Mekanni said as he shuddered. *Some things of the past should stay buried.*

She simply nodded and continued walking, staring at the ground.

Mekanni could sense the great pain and sadness in her heart, but he said nothing. He did not want to know what else happened the night he first gained the sickness, for what he knew was enough to know Delsenni abandoned him in shame. Though truthfully it was only a temporary abandonment, and Delsenni had more than made up to him for it, it still resonated within his heart as if it was another sickness. Delsenni abandoned him. Delsenfi would never abandon him, though.

Leyrkan Mekanni, we are here, Senraeno said, snapping him back to the present.

The Leyrkan shook his head a few times. If he did not love Delsenni a great deal, he would have cursed her for bringing up the forbidden subject again. This was not the time to become sick again. *Thank you, Senraeno.*

Are you sure you're okay, sir?

Just try to hit that rock again. Envision it as the Fire Queen threatening Jena and everyone else you care about. Pretend that when that rock is finished attacking you, it will slowly destroy everyone you love.

This brought new anger to Senraeno's eyes, and he nodded before he and Jena ran up the hill again.

Mekanni could tell there was going to be something strange about this particular flight, but he could not determine what that was. There was Senraeno, positioning himself for flight as usual. His takeoff was excellent, even by an adult Onizard's standards, but it was nothing unusual for Senraeno, for Mekanni's training had paid off. Senraeno swooped down by the rock, as usual, and then came the jet stream of water that completely destroyed the rock and part of the land around it.

Mekanni could barely believe it; he glanced over at Delsenni and saw her staring at where the rock had been in complete disbelief. Even Jena and Senraeno were shocked, though Senraeno recovered from his shock quickly and walked back over to Mekanni.

Senraeno, since when could you do that? Mekanni asked.

Since I got angry at the Fire Queen for the things she has done. I imagined the rock was her, like you said, and it just happened. I can go find a new rock for you.

Yes, please do that, said Mekanni.

As the Bonds wandered off toward the edge of the clearing to find a new rock, Mekanni shuddered for a new reason. *Why am I sad that he is doing so well?*

He still needs you, Mek. I need you too.

Mekanni stared at the ground. *He won't need me forever.*

That is the way it is with children, dear. But he still loves you as much as he loves his own father. Perhaps he loves you even more than his own father.

I know. I can feel it, Senni, and it scares me. I have failed everyone I have loved; I do not want to fail Senraeno as well.

Nonsense, you have not failed anyone. Such talk will make you sick again.

Mekanni sighed. He knew his mate was right about the sickness, but he could not bring himself to admit it. *It's funny; I always wanted a son, and you, I think, secretly wanted a daughter. Now we have both a son and a daughter.*

Yes, we do, Delsenni said as she embraced him.

The Bonds returned a short time later. Senraeno was carrying the new rock on his back, looking rather pleased at the new find, while Jena was simply smiling at Mekanni and Delsenni.

"We found the rock, Leyrkan and Lady."

I hope it's big enough.

It's perfect, Mekanni said as he looked up at the stars. *Everything is perfect.*

Chapter 30

Come in, Delbralfi said to Bryn, a month after the Teltrena-carrying incident. *I have something to show you.*

"This had better not be imminent death," the human said.

Certainly not; it's a new place for you to live. Delbralfi said as he led Bryn toward the shadows in the back of the leyr.

I helped build it, Deldenno added.

Delbralfi grinned as he sensed his Bond's pride. *It has been here for a while, but we had to enlarge it, since you are a bigger human than its last occupant.*

"It's a room in the middle of your wall."

Yes, and we can simply roll a large boulder in front of the doorway and the Fire Queen will not notice a thing.

Bryn's eyes widened, and he ran toward the entrance again. "You're not trapping me in there to suffocate! Fire Queen or no Fire Queen, I don't need that kind of false friendship."

Bral and I have been planning it for months now. Even Idenno helped with its design, Deldenno said, bowing his head in disappointment.

There is an air hole in one of the sides. It is hidden by the rock for the time being, but it is there.

"The washed-up Watchzard with no life helped you build it? That makes me feel a thousand times better, guys. I think I'll go in there right now and let you trap me in there. While you're roasting me, maybe you should throw some clay in there and make new cleaning buckets for your next slave."

Bryn, I thought you were getting better about trusting us, Delbralfi said. *We expanded the hiding place for a reason.*

"Well, a man has to have his limits somewhere, and being shoved into a hole in the wall is mine."

Bryn, it's for your protection, Delbralfi protested. *We heard the Fire Queen is planning to-*

Enforce my punishment, she said, as she entered the leyr. *But it seems I shall have to create more punishments, if this is the true nature of my son.*

My queen, I-

No more lies, Delbralfi. I knew it could not be a coincidence that Senme has become the most cheerful human in the Sandleyr. You are not keeping the humans in their place.

Yes, I am, the younger Child of Fire said. *Human beings are our equals. Perhaps they are even greater than us, for while you have killed many humans, no human has ever murdered an Onizard.*

Human beings are weaker than us; that is why they cannot murder an Onizard, just as they cannot Bond. Your selfish attempt to prove they could only served to get rid of an efficient slave.

Delbralfi tore his claws into the ground in anger. *Jena was more than a slave, you demon! She was far greater than you will ever be!*

Demon? The Fire Queen smirked as if she was hiding her anger. *If I am a demon, you are the child of demons. Do not disgrace your own blood; you are the descendant of a great Queen of the Onizards, and you cannot let your precious Teltrena forget it.*

Delbralfi's anger turned to fear. *What did you say?*

You cannot possibly think I did not notice the way you got along so nicely with her. It is a perfect match; I approve of it greatly. I watched the way you were always talking to her these past months, and I saw you carry her to her leyr one night while I was trying to investigate a crime that has happened in the Sandleyr. I hope that you enjoyed yourself, and I also hope that she did not put up too much of a struggle.

I would never dishonor her like that!

Of course not, the Fire Queen rolled her eyes as if she didn't believe him. *Why dishonor her, when you can force her to become your joinmate for life? Teltrena is a weakling who fears me greatly; if you simply put her in her place, she will fear you as well. You will be able to do whatever you like with her, and when I die, she will be the perfectly subservient queen to a powerful Fire King.*

No! Delbralfi screamed. *I would never do that to her. When you are gone, the Sandleyr shall rejoice as Rulsaesan takes her rightful place as ruler of this Sandleyr. I am content to remain Delbralfi, and nothing else. I do not even claim the title of your son.*

So Rulsaesan, humans, and a non-nature have a hold over your heart. I expected this kind of treachery from other Onizards, but not from you. It seems I did not put you in your place enough as a child, she said in an eerily calm tone. Then, with one quick motion, she jabbed him underneath the eye with her front horn. Her horn did not break, though the gash was deep.

Delbralfi fell back, wincing in pain as he felt his blood begin to ooze from the wound. He refused to step away from Bryn, though; no one was going to die if he had any say in the situation.

I believe your lady friend will never consider you as anything now that you have that wound. When it becomes a hideous scar like mine, it will constantly remind her of her own failure, of who you are, and of what your destiny is in life.

Delbralfi refused to cry in front of the Fire Queen. *A scar is just a scar; it does not dictate my destiny. My destiny is here, protecting Bryn and Deldenno. You can kill me if you wish, but it will not hide the fact that you have failed. I am not your son.*

Then I shall not be your mother! The Fire Queen screamed as she attempted to knock him down with her tail.

Delbralfi parried the blow with his own tail, only to feel the terrible kick of defeat. The Fire Queen had broken his front leg with her own front leg, and now, losing his balance, Delbralfi fell to the ground, and Deldenno was rendered helpless by feeling the pain through their link.

You are lucky I am not allowed to kill you, The Fire Queen said calmly as she stepped over and broke one of his back legs.

Delbralfi screamed in agony.

Weakness is in your blood, it seems. Now that your rebellious nature is calmed for the time being, I shall take the human to his punishment. The Fire Queen said as she held her tail to Bryn's throat, her tail flame inches away from burning him right there.

I am sorry, Bryn, Delbralfi said.

"Bral, you are my friend," he said softly, before the Fire Queen forced him forward.

Go forward and face your fate, Senme, she said.

Chapter 31

Bryn took one last look around the Invitation Hall before the Fire Queen forced him to move forward. He could see that there were several Onizards watching him, but none of them showed any real concern. It seemed that Bryn was truly dying alone.

"So this is it," he mumbled to himself. "I only hope Delbralfi lives to remember Jena and I," he added, resisting the great urge to look back toward where he had come. If he looked back, those apathetic Onizards would believe he was afraid to die. Bryn was not afraid to die; he was afraid to let his memory of Jena die with him.

Jena's death had come as a complete shock to him; she had lived so long and so well, he had almost thought she was invincible. Even now, he thought he saw her standing on one of the ledges high above. But he knew he was just hallucinating before his death, for when he looked closely she was gone again. When he was dead, no one would remember her name.

"Unless..." Bryn said softly as an idea came to him. He looked about at the Onizards now gathering to watch his execution, and smiled.

Keep walking, scum, the Fire Queen said, pushing him forward a few steps.

"Jena's star is the brightest in the heavens!" Bryn shouted as loudly as he could.

Silence! Humans do not have stars!

"I shall not stay silent anymore, while I still live to tell of Jena! You've run out of threats, Fire Queen; you're already going to kill me," Bryn said as he laughed in defiance of the Onizard. "All of you can only dream of having a star bright enough to outshine Jena's, for in spite of your demon queen, she smiled."

Silence! the Fire Queen shrieked again.

"Very well, Queen of Scum, I shall say no more, for no words can describe the courage, strength, and kindness of Jena," Bryn said as he turned around to face her. "You don't scare me at all."

The Fire Queen lowered her head and scowled at him. *You will be scared when you burn alive, screaming for someone to put you out of your misery, desperate to end your pathetic excuse for a life. Then, I am certain you would deny your precious Jena simply to end your own suffering.*

"Never," Bryn said, though his voice wavered more than he wished it would as he closed his eyes. Now that he was standing outside of the Fire Queen's leyr, he could only wait for the terrible flame breath of the Fire Queen he had heard so much about.

It never came. Instead, Bryn heard the flutter of wings and several loud thuds. When he opened his eyes, a strange, golden Onizard was standing in front of him, facing the Fire Queen with her wings unfurled. It appeared she had knocked the Fire Queen aside with the orb on the end of her tail, which she was now holding carefully over the Fire Queen's head. Bryn had heard of the Child of Light Rulsaesan, but he did not expect such a mysterious and quiet Onizard to come to his rescue.

The killing ends today, Deybralfi, Rulsaesan said.

You cannot stop me; I am Fire Queen! You are just the last of an ancient race of Onizards doomed for extinction.

Doomed for extinction? You do not remember what your mother taught you, do you? The Children of Light have the powers of empathy because they are protectors of the heart of the Sandleyr. If you say there will be no more of us left after I die, you are in essence saying that the entire Sandleyr is doomed for extinction.

You do not have the heart of the Sandleyr under your control, Rulsaesan.

Neither do you, The Lady of Day said. From the way she spoke, Bryn imagined she was smiling. *Yet everyone controls one piece of the Sandleyr's heart, even the humans like this boy. I cannot let the Sandleyr lose more of its heart anymore.*

The Sandleyr will be a better place after his death.

I will be the judge of that, Rulsaesan said as she finally lifted her tail away from the Fire Queen's head. *Ammasan's heir will come one day, and then I will have the power to banish you for good. In the meantime, there is to be no more death in the*

Sandleyr. No law gives you the power to kill, especially not those you consider weaker than you.

I can make a new law. I am Fire Queen, Deybralfi said, though she had less conviction in her words.

Only the Leyrque can make true laws, Deybralfi, Rulsaesan said. *And you are no Leyrque. Begone, and leave everyone in peace for a while. You're acting like a child who ate all the sweet grass and started craving the sweet grass of others.*

The Fire Queen gave one last glare at Bryn and Rulsaesan before stomping across the Invitation Hall back to her leyr. *You will pay for this, Rulsaesan.*

No, but I would have paid for it had I not done something, the Child of Light said before she turned to Bryn. *Are you okay?*

"I'm fine," he said, "Surely you should know that though, Lady Rulsaesan."

I was just trying to be polite, she said as she laughed. *Come, I will take you someplace safer for both of us.*

"What about Delbralfi?" Bryn asked before he realized there were still Onizards watching, curious about the Child of Light speaking to a mere human. He lowered his voice to a whisper as he said, "The Fire Queen hurt him...he risked his life for me."

Rulsaesan paused for a moment, closing her eyes as if she were intensely concentrating on something. Then, she began to laugh, and Bryn had to wonder about her sanity.

"Lady Rulsaesan, is Delbralfi okay?"

Do not worry; Delbralfi is fine. Come, you must be hungry.

Chapter 32

Teltrena watched Rulsaesan confront the Fire Queen and smiled. Before Senraeno was born, she would not have cared about a random human death, but now her heart had changed. Part of her wished that she had been the one to confront the Fire Queen, but she knew that Rulsaesan had greater influence and power than she did. Only Rulsaesan would be able to protect the boy; Teltrena was content for the time being to quietly rebel. Lost in thought, her mind drifted to Delbralfi and how happy he would be when he found out that his human friend was safe again. It was miraculous that he hadn't done anything to stop Bryn from being taken away in the first place.

Or perhaps he had. Teltrena stood up in fear as she considered this possibility. Delbralfi would have tried to use his influence as the Fire Queen's son to stop her, and he would not have just let Bryn go without a fight. Even Deldenno would have tried to do something, as powerless as the young Onizard was. As she looked as closely as she could at the Fire Queen's horn, she noticed fresh blood dripping down. Horrified, Teltrena wondered if there was a real death in the Sandleyr today.

The non-nature knew there was only one path for her now. The others would have to rely on their own resources to survive or die; her heart was one of a Child of Earth, and there was an injured Onizard who needed her help.

Teltrena flew quickly to Delbralfi's leyr, unnoticed by all of the Onizards gathering to see the strange confrontation. She entered cautiously, hoping that she was not too late.

Lady Tel, his legs and eye hurt really badly, Deldenno said, walking slowly to the back of the leyr to show her. His voice was comforting, even though he sounded like he was in great pain, for it reassured Teltrena that her kind and sweet friend had not died.

When she actually saw the Child of Fire, though, Teltrena gasped in horror. Two of Delbralfi's legs were broken, and he had a deep gash under his eye that was bleeding profusely. The healing of the legs would be no problem at all; Teltrena had already broken the rules of non-natures once, and that was with an Onizard she didn't care about nearly as much as she cared about Delbralfi. The eye wound, however, brought terror to her heart. Teltrena knew the terrible price he'd pay if she couldn't heal that wound, and she feared that consequence greatly. Delbralfi was too good of an Onizard to deserve the fate of a terrible scar.

Teltrena? Delbralfi asked as he tried to hide his face from her. *Forgive me for the terrible pun, but you're a sight for a sore eye.*

The non-nature smirked. *Well, let's make sure it doesn't stay sore.*

Delbralfi's normally brown eyes had turned lavender. *No, Teltrena, don't risk your life for me. I'm sure it will heal in time.*

It will heal right now, she said, ignoring the strange change in eye color for the time being. *Just close your eyes and relax. I will take care of you.*

The Child of Fire smiled gratefully. *Close your eyes as well, Deldenno. We don't want to give the Fire Queen any witnesses.*

After the child had closed his eyes, Teltrena cautiously healed Delbralfi's legs first. As she suspected, it was an easy task for her powers, and she was grateful she hadn't had a weird vision like the last time she had healed without permission. Each time she used her healing powers, it got easier for her, but she still paused when she came to the eye wound.

It seemed so similar to the Fire Queen's wound had been the dark morning when she became a non-nature, yet it was vastly different in many ways. Before, Teltrena had been practically threatened to heal an Onizard who seemed too suspiciously quiet about how she had gotten the wound. Before, Teltrena had been uncomfortable and afraid, but now she was healing an Onizard out of her own free will, without the instructions and pressures from the Watchzard, from Deyraeno, or from the Fire Queen.

She would not heal anyone else, for even in her desire for rebellion she remained a cautious non-nature. If anyone else had been so brutally injured by the Fire Queen, she would have had the common sense to simply refer him or her to a brave

Child of Earth. Even now, she could easily get a real Child of Earth to heal Delbralfi. In his distrust for them, Delbralfi would probably still admit that they were the better healers. Why was she willing to risk her life to heal Delbralfi, anyway?

Tel, are you okay? Delbralfi asked, opening his good eye and looking at her, seemingly full of concern and worry for her sake. *You don't have to do this. I would bear the scar if it makes you uncomfortable to heal it.*

As Teltrena looked him in the eye, she realized the answer to her question; she loved him. She had thought of him as handsome before she knew him well, but she would not have risked her life for a handsome Onizard, since beauty fades quickly. She had felt comforted by his friendship when others had seen her as a mere non-nature, and she had done her best to return his kindness with her own, despite her knowledge that friendships could fade as quickly as they came. Yet now she knew that she did not want this friendship to fade; she wanted to do everything in her power to make it stronger, within reasonable behavior for a respectable Onizard. Here she was, helping him as he had helped her the day she first met; for the first time, she felt she had a true equal.

As she stood there, looking at him in this new light, she knew the old Teltrena would have walked away and let a real Child of Earth heal his injuries. But the old Teltrena was a selfish fool. She would rather see a smile on his face than let any of his suffering continue when she could do something.

No other Onizard had ever made her feel this way, and she was worried now, for she knew there was no way he could possibly love her in return. Even if he did have similar feelings for her, no one could love a non-nature; it was illegal long before the Fire Queen declared Teltrena was one of them. She couldn't even tell him of her feelings; if the Sandleyr population learned that she loved him, he would be shamed for life. The thought made her extremely upset, but she dismissed her emotions as best as she could as she focused on the job at hand.

I'm fine, she said. *Close your eye again.*

Once his eye was closed, Teltrena gently touched the wound with her tail and let her powers do the work. The skin returned to its original state, and his face looked perfectly normal. There was not even a trace of the wound that had been there before.

You look good as new, Bral! Deldenno said excitedly.

His Bond stood up carefully, as if he were afraid he'd fall again, then he looked at Teltrena and smiled.

Thank you, Teltrena. I am grateful for your help.

It was nothing, Teltrena said. *That is what a friend is for.*

She smiled for a moment as she looked at him, then shyly looked toward the ground. *Well, I suppose I'd better leave before the Fire Queen gets suspicious.*

Oh...yes, he replied, looking almost distraught. *Well, I suppose I'll see you soon?*

Of course, Teltrena said. She would never consider leaving him alone for long. She was Delbralfi's friend, and he was more than a mere friend in her heart. She only regretted being unable to tell him.

Chapter 33

Rulsaesan grinned as she walked back to her leyr, glancing back every few seconds to make sure Bryn had not run away. Strange things were certainly happening in the Sandleyr, but she could not complain. She felt extremely happy, and she could not explain why. To say something now would likely ruin things for many Onizards and humans.

"Lady Rulsaesan, can I ask you something?"

Certainly, Bryn.

"Why couldn't you stand up for yourself before? And why did you rescue me now? Why couldn't you rescue any humans before me?"

The Lady of Day sighed. *There are many reasons, Bryn. For many years, I could not control my powers of empathy. I could feel the joy and happiness of those around me, but I could also feel the pain without any ability to ignore it if I so chose. The Fire Queen knew this, and if I had tried to rescue anyone then, I would have only caused them to die sooner and more painfully.*

"So you've learned how to control your powers now?"

Yes and no. They are still there, and I can't get rid of them, but they do not affect me as greatly as they did before. I can sense that you have some fear of me. You are smart, Bryn, but you do not need to stress yourself by worrying needlessly.

"Then what changed?"

I have gotten stronger somehow. I believe it means that there will be another Child of Light soon to share my burden.

"Then you will rule the Sandleyr, and hopefully bring certain improvements to the policies of your people."

Like the end of using humans as slave labor? Of course; the Fire Queen's proof is all completely false anyway.

The two stepped into Rulsaesan's leyr before Bryn continued, "It is true, though, that humans cannot Bond."

Where do you get an idea like that? Rulsaesan was amused that Bryn still hadn't figured out the truth after working in Delbralfi's leyr and seeing Alair the Onizac every day. *I'm sure some Onizard hatchling is going to chose you as his or her Bond, just to prove how wrong you are.*

Bryn paused for a moment. "Well, it's never happened, and probably never will."

If that is so, why did one of my children Invite Jena?

Bryn seemed shocked. "If she was Invited, then could that hatchling have been-"

It isn't good to speculate on what might have been, Rulsaesan said in an attempt to draw the discussion away from Jena. She was glad that the boy was finally thinking, but she didn't need him to talk about what he was thinking. *Until we know the full truth, it is not right to make judgements on a situation, even if it is a situation that happened in the past.*

"How do you learn the full truth, Rulsaesan?"

By truly listening to others without the prejudice of your own heart. That is what my mentor Ammasan taught me. I hope you have learned that lesson with Delbralfi.

"I have. All this time he was telling me the truth about his loyalties, and I thought he was just trying to betray me to his mother. I should not have listened to the rumors."

Rumors can be useful, as long as you do not believe them. I could start a rumor that I am sick and dying, spread it around the Sandleyr, and regain the rest of my strength before some fool tries to challenge me, Rulsaesan explained. *All you need to do is control what the world sees. The world always saw the bright and cheerful little girl without any fears, but it sometimes it made me nearly cry when I saw her walking by, hiding her sadness in her smile.*

"You mean Jena was actually depressed all the time?"

No, she is not. Most of the time, she was not faking her happiness, especially not the times she was with you or Delbralfi. But no soul can truly be happy all the time, even a girl as strong as Jena is.

"Was," Bryn sighed.

What? Rulsaesan said, feigning shock. *Oh yes, of course I meant was. Forgive me, it has been a long day, Bryn, and you must be hungry. I will bring you some sweet grass.*

"You stole sweet grass?"

Of course not, Rulsaesan laughed. *It was given to me as a gift.*

"Then you know who stole it!"

I never saw them steal it, so how would I know?

Bryn sighed, throwing his hands up in feigned defeat. "I give up trying to keep up with all of the conspiracies."

Rulsaesan placed some sweet grass in his hands as she said, *You can't give up; you're aware of them all, so you are the greatest of conspirators.*

"Yes, I am the great conspirator Senme! My greatest conspiracy is my sad attempt to mind my own business."

Ah, but the business of the Sandleyr is your business. You are just as much a part of it as I am.

"But you actually have the abilities to figure out what's going on. You can read the minds of others; I only have the limited use of my brain."

That is no limit, Bryn; your intelligence is greater than the intelligence of many of the Onizards and humans around us. The only limit you have is your temper and your heart.

"But the heart is our greatest strength!"

The heart is everyone's greatest strength, but without rationality, the heart would be useless. If all we relied on was our hearts, you would have been shouting Jena's name too much and too often for me to be of any help to you. The heart needs the mind as a balancing force, or else we would all go mad when we could not get what our hearts desired.

"Is that what happened to the Fire Queen?"

Perhaps, though she stopped using her heart long ago, Rulsaesan said as she frowned in disgust. *Unfortunately, her brain is still working, and her mother taught her a great deal about Sandleyr law before she died.*

"Who was her mother?"

Rulsaesan sighed. *Ammasan.*

"But she was a Child of Light! How did she not know that the Fire Queen was going to turn to evil?"

Children of Light are not omniscient, Bryn. Our powers can only sense the emotions of others; we cannot sense the reasoning behind the emotions. Besides, Deybralfi somehow discovered a way to block our powers. Only when she was afraid or angry could we sense any emotion at all. It strains my powers just to sense that, so I stopped trying.

"That really is horrible," Bryn said. "I still wish you could have helped the others who were hurt by her."

So do I, Bryn. Rulsaesan said as she chewed thoughtfully on a piece of sweet grass. *More than you know.*

Chapter 34

Jena and Senraeno awoke that night to the sound of screaming coming from the Sandleyr entrance. Jena could tell the scream was not human, and she wondered what was going on.

Jena, Senraeno, I need your help, Delsenni said, her voice full of desperation. *Mekanni's sickness has gotten worse.*

Jena climbed up Senraeno's tail, and he carried her to the entrance as quickly as he could. When they arrived, they discovered Delsenni attempting to calm down Mekanni. He was lying prone and trembling violently, screaming seemingly random things about eyes.

He tried to walk to the Watchzard rock to wait for you two for training, and he fell down, Delsenni explained. Her voice trembled as if she was forcing herself to remain calm.

The eyes! Mekanni screamed. *Don't let them get me, Senfi!*

Senfi is here, my dear Mek. The eyes are gone now, Delsenni said before turning to Jena and Senraeno. *He's having a full attack and I can't stop it this time. He might have even fallen because of the sickness starting. All I know is that if I try to touch him, he'll go even more berserk.*

The eyes can't have me...only Delsenfi can, the Leyrkan of Night mumbled.

"Lord Mekanni, the eyes aren't here anymore," Jena said as comfortingly as she could, reaching out to pat his shoulder. "Your mate Delsenni is right here."

My mate is Delsenfi, and only Delsenfi! Mekanni screamed. *That Delsenni is an impostor, and probably on the side of the eyes! Delsenfi, help me!*

Delsenfi is here, my Mek, the Child of Night said, holding back her tears as she watched her mate struggle.

Mekanni began sobbing. *Delsenfi, I love you.* he said, clearly not seeing anything in the present. *I tried to stop the eyes, but I couldn't. Don't leave me, Delsenfi!*

Jena attempted to calm down the Leyrkan of Night by wiping some of the sweat off of his face.

Jena, no! He can't control his power to show memories when he's sick! shouted Delsenni. It was too late, however, because Mekanni in his delirium had begun to show her what he was seeing.

The night was young, and Idenno was dancing. Mekanni could not help laughing at the Child of Water as he pranced about the Sandleyr entrance, occasionally impersonating other Onizards in the middle of one of his elaborate dance steps.

This Sandleyr is full of useless beings, he stated, curling his lower lip and speaking in what Jena recognized as a bad imitation of the Fire Queen's mental voice. *The humans can't fly like me, the Children of Light boss me around, and the Children of Water get my precious tail wet! Honestly, how can they live anywhere near me?* At the sound of thunder, he added, *Storms are evil as well, for they prevent me from escaping the useless beings.*

You shouldn't mock the Leyrque of Day's daughter, Mekanni said, trying to remain dignified.

Why not? She can't hurt the Lord of Night's only brother and the son of Leyrque Senmani.

Yes, she can. She knows that anger and pain will hurt me, and that will hurt you.

But she is only one Onizard; she can't muster enough anger to hurt you, and even she's not stupid enough to hurt herself.

Mekanni sighed and shook his head. *I suppose you are right.*

Hey now, there's something else worrying you, Mek. What's wrong?

Just stress, I suppose. I'm nervous about being a good father. The child of Delsenfi deserves the best father in the Sandleyr.

Mek, if any of our group would make a good father, you would, Idenno said firmly, though his dance abruptly stopped as he added, *You're the luckiest Onizard in the Sandleyr, Mek. You're the joinmate of the one you love.*

Mekanni looked at his brother worriedly. Ever since Rulsaesan had become the joinmate of Deyraeno, he had acted differently, almost older than his years. He wasn't the same jovial Iden that Mekanni had grown up with. *Being a joinmate isn't necessarily the one proof of all love. You did the right thing by letting her choose Deyraeno. She's happy with him, and I'm certain she wants you to be happy as well.*

Idenno shrugged. Mekanni could tell he was attempting to hide the sadness he felt. *Ah, don't worry about me. I'm going to be an uncle soon! I can't wait to see my new niece or nephew. Do you know what the name is going to be?*

Delsenfi thought it would be good to name the child after the great Leyrkan Senbralni.

Delbral, eh? Let's just hope no one thinks he or she was named after Deybralfi.

With Delsenfi, the most beautiful Onizard in the Sandleyr, as his mother? I highly doubt that.

As the brothers laughed, Mekanni sensed the terrible pain normally only associated with a death in the Sandleyr. Worried, he looked to Iden. *I think there's something wrong, there's-*

Oh my Lord of the Sky! Ammasan! Don't die on me! cried their mother. *She's attacking! Oh, Lord of the Sky, Ammasan is dead! Stars protect us!*

Eyes widening, Mekanni said, *Iden, go wake Deyraeno up.*

There is no way I'm going to leave you when I hear Mom screaming like that! Don't do anything stupid, Mek!

Iden, don't argue with me. If this murderer killed Ammasan, she'll go after Rulsaesan. I need you to protect her and Deyraeno!

That ended all arguments with Idenno. *Good luck. Come back alive.*

I will, he said, but there was doubt in his heart.

As Mekanni flew into the Sandleyr to face whoever or whatever was attacking, he used his mental strength to tell Delsenfi, *Protect our egg. If I don't come back, know that I love you.*

Mekanni landed on the Invitation Hall floor and shuddered in terror at the sight before him. Deybralfi was standing with the full weight of her front legs on his mother's throat, and the Child of Fire's back legs were pinning Senmani's tail down, preventing the Leyrque from defending herself from death by suffocation. Yet Senmani did not show any sign of fear, until her gaze fell upon her son.

Mekanni...leave this place! Senmani choked. *I'm done for; escape to your family.*

There is no escape from me, Deybralfi sneered, dragging her claws playfully on the Leyrque's throat.

Stop this! Mekanni shouted. *Let her go!*

With pleasure! Go off to the stars, Leyrque of Night! Smiling with malice, Deybralfi slit Senmani's throat with her claws.

Mekanni was hit with the full force of pain that came with death, made worse by the fact he was in close proximity when it happened. He fell to the ground and struggled in pain from Senmani's death, and he found to his horror that he did not have the strength to stand up against Deybralfi and all of the hatred that she had unleashed. All the hope and the love of the sleeping Sandleyr was no match for the terror of her utterly soulless gaze. He could sense no inner kindness, no love, and no remorse inside of the Child of Fire. She only had the will to murder, and it seemed that Mekanni was going to be chosen as the next victim.

Pathetic, the foul Child of Fire sneered as she kicked sand into Mekanni's eyes. As his eyes teared up and he attempted to clear the painful cloud of sand away from his eyes, she added, *I had hoped the great Lord of Night would put up more of a struggle than this. I was supposed to kill you after a glorious fight.* With an accusatory glare, she stormed out of Mekanni's field of vision.

He trembled from fear of the unknown before he felt a sudden, searing pain all through his front left leg. He felt her grip tighten on the leg, and as he screamed in agony he prayed she would not completely tear it off.

Had enough already, Lord of Night? She asked, her mental voice stronger and louder as she held her head above him, making certain that he looked into her soulless eyes.

Why are you doing this? He asked, through gasps of pain.

You fool, she laughed, letting go of his mutilated leg and pacing away out of his line of vision again. *The Children of Light have always held the power and respect in the Sandleyr, taking for granted their blessings. When you are all dead, the Sandleyr will be in chaos as the Onizards try to find a new authority; who better than Deybralfi, daughter of the last Leyrque of Day?*

You monster! They will never accept you as Queen! Mekanni cried, though he did not know if he spoke the truth. Who would suspect her of killing her own mother?

Mekanni felt her talons claw into his back left leg and bit back a scream as she tore it out of its socket. Laughing, she slowly walked back into his field of vision, carrying his barely-attached back leg most of the way.

Why should you care, Lord of Night? she asked, spitting in his face after saying "Lord of Night". *You shall not live to see my reign.* But no matter, she said, a sudden grin appearing as she eyed Mekanni's vulnerable, mutilated body as if he were an interesting object her attacks had perfected. A glimmer of something even more terrifying than pure hatred appeared in her eyes. *I will make sure your line lives on, even after I kill you.*

Mekanni trembled violently as he realized the meaning of her words. *No, please...Help! Delsenfi! Anyone! Please!*

No one will answer to you anymore, the fire demon said, coming uncomfortably closer with each word. *Not even your precious Delsenfi. You are a useless Leyrkan to a Sandleyr that will hate you. No one will hear your cries for help, and I shall enjoy this night even more.*

Yet he still screamed for help with all that was left of his strength, and the great feelings of fear, pain, and shame remained in his memory, even though everything after the Fire Queen's words was nothing but blackness and the terrible, lustful hatred of the eyes.

Jena stood in shock, hardly believing what she had just seen and felt. She did not realize she was crying until Senraeno gently wiped her tears away with his tail. Then as she broke down and began sobbing, she held his tail tightly as she watched the Leyrkan of Night slowly rise to his feet.

Mekanni turned to Delsenni and said nothing for a long time as she let him lean on her shoulder. Jena could see he was trying to avoid being seen crying, even if she had inadvertently seen his darkest of memories. After an agonizing minute, he turned to Jena and said, *I am sorry about what happened to your mother, Jena.*

"How do you know about that?" Jena asked fearfully, though she knew the Child of Light had no desire to betray anyone else's secrets.

You showed me, Mekanni smiled sadly. *Unintentionally, of course, but that is what happens when anyone tries to see another's memories. There is always an exchange,* he said as he lifted Jena's head up with his tail; her fresh tears glistened in the pale light. *I am sorry you had to see that memory, dear child. If I had the power to make you forget it, I would use that power on you, then myself.*

"No, I'm the one who should be sorry, Leyrkan. You have enough pain without seeing the cause of mine."

Jena, I am glad we understand each other's sorrows at last. If anything, you have given me a wonderful gift in your memory.

"How could that memory be a gift?"

You have a very good friend in Delbralfi, Mekanni answered, taking a sudden interest in the stars. *I am glad the rumors I hear about him being like his mother aren't true.*

Delsenni sighed and took a sudden interest in the ground.

For a long moment, Jena simply looked at Mekanni as she examined him in a new and unexpected way. "Your eyes...they weren't always lavender, were they?"

Mekanni closed his eyes and turned his head away from everyone as if to hide his great and terrible shame. *No. Once, long ago, they were dark brown. But I fear the stress that causes them to remain lavender will never go away. I hope nothing causes my son's eyes to stay lavender forever.*

"Delbralfi's eyes are brown; he's a good Onizard, mostly happy in spite of his circumstances."

I will never know that for certain. Deybralfi has told everyone that I'm a pathetic Onizard, driven mad by the early death of mother. I did not want a son with that demon; I would have willed Delsenni's Delbral to live, but I do not want my all of my chances of being a good father destroyed. Of all the pain I've felt, losing my children was the worst pain possible.

Losing your child, Delsenni said quietly as she looked toward the stars, avoiding looking everyone in the eyes.

"You haven't lost him; he's—what?"

Delsenni bit her lip and struggled vainly before she burst into tears of her own. *Mek, please forgive me. I had to protect him from that monster!*

Senni, who did you have to protect from that monster?

Delsenni sighed. *Jena, touch my head at the same time as Mekanni. I want to transfer this memory only once.*

Jena and Mekanni stepped forward together and reached out cautiously. They closed their eyes and opened them in Delsenni's memory.

Delsenfi and her egg were safely hidden inside the mother's leyr that was attached to the Leyr Grounds. It was raining, and a considerable amount of time had passed since Mekanni spoke those cryptic words to her. Delsenfi shivered from cold and worry for her love. Then she saw Senmani walking toward her.

There was at once peace and sadness in her eyes as she walked toward Delsenfi. She was barely visible, even taking into consideration the Child of Fire's relatively poor vision standards at night. Her tail did not even emit any light. Delsenfi stifled a cry as the Leyrque came closer; the rain was falling through Senmani instead of onto her. With each step she took, Senmani faded more and more.

Are you...?

Dead? Senmani finished for her. *Yes, I am. But my son still lives, and you must save him. You are the only one who can now.*

The rain will kill me! And what will happen to my child?

Rain cannot kill a Child of Light, Delsenni, The former Leyrque sighed as she looked one last time toward the Sandleyr entrance. *Your love will keep you both strong when all else fails. Never forget that; your lives depend on it. Your child will be safe, despite whatever you may see tonight; rescue his father now!*

As Senmani faded away for good, Delsenni shuddered in sudden pain. The minor pain of her body changing to that of a Child of Light was nothing compared to the emotional torment of hearing her beloved Mekanni screaming for her at the same time as she was feeling every bit of his pain.

Stay strong, she said to herself, carefully covering her egg partially with sand. *Mother will be back soon,* she said to Delbral before she unfurled her wings and flew into the rain for the first time in her life.

Her fastest flying speed wasn't fast enough for her as she flew to the Sandleyr entrance, her heart burning with fear and hatred for the creature who had done this to her family. When she could see Mekanni's prone form, she was horrified to discover what Deybralfi was doing to him, and her rage grew all the more potent. Before Deybralfi even had time to react to her presence, Delsenni had knocked her off Mekanni and stabbed her in the eye with her front horn, breaking a piece off the top in the process. She knew a Child of Light was supposed to show mercy, but she did not feel like showing mercy to a monster. *Leave this Sandleyr, if you know what's good for you. I will kill you if you come any closer to me or those I care about!*

Deybralfi's eyes showed traces of fear and pain, yet Delsenni could sense no remorse or care in the Child of Fire. Deybralfi smiled haughtily as she said, *We shall see who wins in the end. I have more power over you than you will ever have over me.*

As the fire demon flew away, Delsenni began speaking to Mekanni tenderly, hoping that the terror and pain in his now-lavender eyes would go away. *Mek, it's me. It's your Delsenfi. She's gone now. You don't need to worry anymore; I shall protect you.*

Delsenfi, I'm sorry, Mekanni sobbed. *I couldn't stop her. She...*

Don't think of it anymore. She's gone, and she can't hurt us anymore. Idenno will be here soon with a Child of Earth, and I will go guard our egg.

The rest...they're safe from the eyes? the Leyrkan of Night trembled violently. *Don't let the eyes get them!*

Of course, Mek. I will protect everyone from the eyes, Delsenni assured him even as she worried that she couldn't. What had Deybralfi meant when she spoke of who would win in the end?

As she flew outside, Delsenni noticed the rain had stopped. What had once been her curse was now a source of protection that had vanished into the night like an empty promise. Her eyes drifted up to the Leyr Grounds and her greatest of fears.

Utter terror paralyzed Delsenni as she watched the demonic Onizard hold her egg over the wall of the Leyr Grounds. Nothing would be able to survive a fall from that height, and there was nothing she could do to stop Delbral's egg from shattering, even if she flew underneath to catch him. There was nothing but her egg, crowned with light from Deybralfi's tail flame, and the cruel eyes staring intently at her, gleaming with malice that told her one step closer would kill any hope she had for the future.

You have already killed innocent Onizards. If you harm an unhatched egg, the Onizards in the Day Kingdom will find you guilty and banish you as I have, she said, though her voice was robbed of its commanding tone.

Oh, I have no intention of destroying the egg, the Fire Queen turned her head away from Delsenni as if she were an unimportant nuisance. *I would not kill my own child.*

No! Delsenni screamed, *You have already caused Mekanni enough pain. I will not let you take our child from us!*

I believe you will, and you will swear it is my child, if you want it to survive, Deybralfi said. *I could drop the egg right now and feel no guilt from doing so. I really should, after that nasty wound you gave me. But I told your joinmate I would keep his line alive, and I do not want to disappoint the Leyrkan of Night.*

All of Delsenni's pain and utter anger came out in her sobs.

Do not worry, I will take good care of my child. Naturally, I am saddened by the tragedy that your own child never hatched, but my child will have nothing to do with you, At once the terrible eyes Mekanni had spoken of turned to the Lady of Night. *If you attempt to contact him, or tell anyone what happened here tonight, I will prove to you that your own child is dead. You will hear its screams before I silence them, and then if I'm feeling particularly generous I will kill you and Mekanni before you die of grief.*

The memory faded to show Delsenni standing in front of them, silently crying as she looked to the ground, her wings hidden against her body in shame. Mekanni seemed completely shocked and close to tears of his own as he looked at his joinmate with this new information in mind.

All this time, my memory was incomplete, and I thought- Mekanni choked back tears. *-I thought you had abandoned me, ashamed of what the demon had done to me.*

Delsenni sobbed. *I could never abandon you, Mek. I love you, and nothing that has happened to you brings me shame. I am the one who should be ashamed; I am the one who failed everyone I love, not you.*

Senni, you did the right thing, Mekanni said. *Do not blame yourself for the actions of that demon who did this to us.*

I could have done something. I should have found some way to protect our egg while I was fighting off that monster! I failed you both.

That is what the demon would want you to think, Senni. You didn't fail us; you could not have been in two places at once, and I would have died if you hadn't shown up when you did.

Idenno would have rescued you.

Idenno is my brother, but he could not rescue me like you did that night. Your love kept me alive and gave me the will to keep living. It kept us all alive when all other strengths failed, Mekanni cautiously pulled his joinmate closer to him as he added, *I am the one who should be sorry for not showing you how much I love you every single night that I live.*

Delsenni's tear-stained smile covered the majority of her face. *You don't need to show me that you love me, Mekanni. Just having the courage to live after what happened to you is enough for me.*

You deserve more than what passes for enough, especially since you are my courage to live. I am the luckiest Onizard alive, and it's about time I started acknowledging it.

"Senraeno and I will leave you alone now, Leyrkan and Lady of Night," Jena said as she bowed to them, trying in vain to hide a grin. "Before I go, though, I'd like to thank you."

For what, Jena? asked Delsenni.

"For Delbralfi. He truly is a good Onizard, and a good friend."

Thank you for helping him become one, Jena. If you ever come out of hiding, please tell our son that we love him.

"Don't worry, I will. I know how important it is to know you are loved."

Chapter 35

Morning came to the Sandleyr, and though it was normally quiet at that early time of day, an occasional sound of crumbling stone echoed across the Invitation Hall.

"Careful, Rae, you'll catch someone's attention," Jena cautioned as her Bond practiced his abilities. The entire leyr was now full of dents in the wall, but Senraeno showed no signs of being tired. Why should he be? He was young, and he was strong, and he certainly wasn't spending any of his youthful energy doing anything else.

Jena, I have to practice now, since I couldn't last night.

"You won't get any more chances for practice if you catch someone's attention."

You certainly caught my attention, Teltrena commented as she entered. A look of shock crossed her face as she looked about the wreck that was the leyr. *What have you been up to? You are going to have to clean this all up yourselves; I have other work to do, and I'm not risking getting caught up here with two renegades.*

I was only practicing, Senraeno said, firing another water blast at the wall. *I want to be prepared if I ever have to fight that fire demon.*

Teltrena stared in awe. *You've learned quickly. Truly the blood of Light flows through your veins.*

"It wasn't really the Light bloodline. It was constant practice under the guidance of Leyrkan Mekanni and Lady Delsenni."

Now you're just telling stories, Teltrena laughed. *I'm sure Mekanni and Delsenni didn't have time to teach you those things. They have a kingdom to rule.*

When there's only two subjects awake in the Night Kingdom, they had plenty of time to spend teaching one of them how to use his powers. Anyway, whether you believe it or not, they taught me.

I suppose I shall have to believe you, Teltrena laughed. *I'll leave you two to practice, but be careful; I don't want you to get caught.*

All Onizards report! the familiar cry of the Fire Queen echoed in everyone's minds.

Teltrena rolled her eyes and sighed. *What does her majesty want now, I wonder? Well, I'd better leave. Even though she considers me equal to the humans, she'll still kill me if I didn't come to these annoying meetings.*

Teltrena flew away and landed in an area where no Onizards were gathering, then turned to watch the Fire Queen from a distance. But the Fire Queen stormed over to the non-nature and glared at her for a full minute, saying nothing.

How may I serve you, my queen? Teltrena asked, her discomfort clear to Senraeno.

Tell me, non-nature, why you have been going up to the abandoned leyr every day for the last six months, sometimes even carrying extra food? I am certain you could not be eating it all yourself.

"We're caught," Jena whispered as she quickly stepped out of view of the Onizards below.

I decided, my Queen, that I would eat up there from now on, as to not disgrace you with my presence, Teltrena lied, avoiding direct eye contact.

I am sure, then, that you wouldn't mind if I had a look to see you hadn't stolen more than your fair share?

Deyraeno shifted uncomfortably. Jena hoped that he had not been noticed, but she realized quickly that it was too much to hope for.

Ah, Deyraeno, perhaps you have something at stake up there.

Of course not, Fire Queen, he lied. *It's just an empty leyr.*

We shall see, said Deybralfi as she took off suddenly, leaving the other Onizards helpless to protect their friends. Quickly Jena and Senraeno found themselves face to face with the cruel stare of the Fire Queen, trapped between her and the edge of the leyr. If either of them moved any further, they would fall to their deaths.

This leyr is hardly empty; it holds a worthless renegade human and an Onizard who was supposed to have been left behind due to his injuries! I say we must think of a suitable punishment for the two traitors who protected them after they watch their treachery be destroyed in front of them.

Jena shuddered in utter terror, desperately looking for a way to rescue herself and Senraeno. But before she had time to think, her Bond decided to speak.

You are wrong, fire demon! No crime has been committed here, for Deyraeno and Teltrena were only aiding a Bonded Onizard and a noble human. I am Senraeno, Bond of the Zarder Jena!

Murmurs echoed throughout the Sandleyr as the other Onizards absorbed the shock of Senraeno's message. Jena would have laughed when she heard Deldenno's cry of *I knew it!* if she had been in a less dangerous position.

I shall kill you, and your pitiful human Bond! With a swift blow, the Fire Queen threw Jena across the leyr. Jena hit the back wall and fell to the ground, regretting as she lost consciousness that her part in the battle was over before it began.

There was no escape for Senraeno now; if he flew away, no one could protect Jena from being brutally slaughtered, and he would fall to his death. But he had no way of getting past the Fire Queen to rescue her, and she would not let him live now that he had revealed his identity as the Bond of a human.

I do not see why you believe I am unjust, the Fire Queen said as she pushed Senraeno closer to the edge. Her eyes sparkled with malice as she watched him shudder. *The Sandleyr has thrived under the belief that you were dead; it is time to make certain it stays thriving.*

Senraeno closed his eyes as he saw her lifting her talons to rip him apart; he would not give the fire demon pleasure by showing her the fear in his eyes. Yet after an agonizing second of waiting in darkness for his death to come, Senraeno's eyes opened in surprise and horror as he heard a familiar but unexpected voice.

Kill me first.

Her voice was soft, but there was no beggar's tone to Teltrena's statement; it was clear and commanding enough to make the Fire Queen pause in her moment of triumph and glare at the non-nature.

You will not spare the child by offering your own pathetic excuse for a life.

I know this, Teltrena said. *I may be a non-nature, but I am no fool. You will take my life, and then you will destroy the child and his Bond. Perhaps you are the real fool, for you cannot understand a simple command; kill me first.*

Teltrena, no! Delbralfi shouted, but she looked him in the eye and shook her head. Senraeno was glad that he did not receive the full strength of her gaze; even watching it from the side, he could see the utter hopelessness in her eyes, despite the grim and determined smile she held as she turned back to the Fire Queen.

You cannot deny that you've wanted to kill me ever since I failed to heal you. You've silently watched me, wondering when I would finally stand up for myself. Losing your power has haunted your dreams, and you've known the only way to protect your power is to kill me. After all, I am the one who made certain that the Zarder and her Bond were fed. My very existence is an insult to your Sandleyr. Why don't you just end it now? Teltrena unfurled her wings and lifted her head proudly, exposing her vulnerable neck and body. *I'm just an insignificant non-nature, so no one will miss me.*

Cautiously, as if waiting for the non-nature to strike at her, the Fire Queen stepped toward Teltrena. When nothing happened, she began to laugh, and the sound of her laughter was harsh on Senraeno's ears. Never before had he heard a sound so cruel, so devoid of emotion. As her laughter continued, the Fire Queen swiftly raised her tail and hit Teltrena with as much effort as if she were swatting at a fly. Then there was nothing but the terrible laughter and the scream Teltrena emitted as she plummeted to the ground, her wings a mere mass of flames.

Teltrena felt the terrible force behind the blow before she felt the flames consuming her. As she lost her balance and tumbled off the ledge, she screamed in spite of her desire to deny the Fire Queen that satisfaction. As she fell, her wings rendered utterly useless, she did not dare to look at the ground below that was certain to claim her life. She saw nothing but the light streaming from the Sandleyr entrance, and only hoped that her fall had distracted the Fire Queen for long enough to give Senraeno a chance to save himself.

Then time seemed to slow down, and a pale figure of an Onizard began walking on the air toward her. Teltrena could see through the ghostly golden form of the other Onizard, but what held her attention were the blue eyes of the mysterious Child of Light. She inspected Teltrena cautiously before she smiled warmly, as if she were gazing at a child who had finally grown to adulthood. Slowly fading away, she spoke one sentence:

Senraeno and Jena are safe now, Teltresan.

Then she vanished as quickly as she had come, and in her place was the form of Delbralfi, Child of Fire, flying to rescue the non-nature from certain death. Though the pain from the burns still tormented her, Tel felt peace for the first time she could remember as she landed in the safety of his wings. Slowly, carefully he carried her to the ground, gently laying her down and grasping her tail in his. Barely conscious, Tel looked into the eyes of the one she loved and smiled.

The last thing she heard before she lost consciousness was Delbralfi urgently saying, *Teltrena, please don't die on me. I-*

The Fire Queen's tail was exposed, and the burning flame taunted Senraeno. He had to put a stop to the cruel laughter; he could not bear the sound of screaming anymore. The opportunity was right; something was distracting the Fire Queen. She had not heard the sound of Teltrena's body hitting the ground with full force, for something had stopped Teltrena's fall. With his remaining strength, the young Onizard swiftly hit the Fire Queen's tail with the full force of his water breath.

Senraeno smiled grimly as he watched her stumble, though fear came to him as she fell to the floor near Jena. After a few brief moments of utter terror, he smiled grimly when he found that he was still alive, and cautiously stood up and walked over to his Bond, ignoring the Fire Queen's shrieks of pain.

Jena stirred from her unconscious state and held onto her right leg, groaning in pain. Senraeno could sense that it was broken, and would have laughed had he not been so worried about his Bond.

"Senraeno, what happened?" she asked as she surveyed her surroundings.

It does not matter. You are safe, for the time being. Of course, when the Fire Queen has the strength to stand again, we shall have to deal with her.

Jena smiled, and stood up on her good leg, using Senraeno to support her weight. Her smile faded, however, when she heard Delbralfi speaking.

Teltrena! Please, don't die on me. I-

-I love you. Delbralfi confessed, not caring who heard him now. He could feel Teltrena's pulse slowing down as he held onto her tail tightly, as if his very grasp would keep her from the inevitable. His own wings and upper body were covered with minor burns, but his physical pain was nothing compared to the pain he felt from looking at the mass of charred flesh that was once her wings. Her eyes were closed and she was smiling, as if she were in a peaceful slumber enjoying a pleasant dream. But if she was breathing at all, she was taking very shallow breaths.

Sobbing, he continued, *I'm so sorry I never told you before now. I was scared that I'd lose you if I said anything. But Bryn was right; forgive me for being too stupid to tell you that I would miss you if you left this world.*

There was no response from the non-nature's prone form, though her pulse continued in a beat too slow for Delbralfi's liking.

Tel? Delbralfi asked, desperately looking about to see if any Child of Earth would do something, anything, to rescue his Teltrena. *Someone help her, please!* But no Onizard moved, save Rulsaesan, who could only shake her head in sadness. Delbralfi turned and glared at his mother in frustration and pain, noting with grim satisfaction how she was helplessly lying on the ground in agony. Surely now she would finally pay for her terrible crimes. Yet this did not comfort him when he heard her speak.

Let her go. It is over. I am still Queen, and you will all be punished as traitors when I stand again.

The scream of rage, pain, and loss that Delbralfi emitted thundered across the Sandleyr as his tears began to fall in rapid succession. He could not give up on her; he refused to lose hope. Yet it seemed his hope was failing forever, and he would truly be a lonely and feared Onizard for the rest of his life. Delbralfi was greatly tempted to let go of her tail and bring justice to the Fire Queen himself. If he killed her now, there was a chance for others to find happiness, even as his happiness was lost to the stars.

Delbralfi! Rulsaesan said in a firm voice that shocked him back to reality. *If you value Teltresan's life, you will not let go until she regains consciousness. It is the Fire Queen's reign that is over.*

Teltresan? Delbralfi gasped as he turned back to see that Teltrena's body was transforming. Her once jade skin was turning to a saffron shade that was at once dark and glowing, and though her charred wings were not completely healed, they were slowly re-forming, the sinews colored with golden yellow. Her horns grew taller and held a green-gold hue, a last tribute to her non-nature form. Delbralfi held onto her tail even tighter than before, and he spoke to her privately.

I always believed in you, Teltresan. Now the whole Sandleyr will be able to see the beauty I long beheld in you.

He could sense that the love he freely gave her was making her stronger. He could feel the steady beat of her heart as the leaf-shaped end of her tail folded in and transformed into the glowing orb of a Child of Light. He could see as she opened her eyes that she was still the same Onizard he loved, and it filled him with unexpected joy.

Delbralfi? Teltresan smiled as she regained consciousness, and then paused as she looked into his eyes, a look of confusion crossing her face. She vainly tried to lift her wings, and cringed from pain.

Someone help the Lady Teltresan's wings! Delbralfi shouted, scanning the crowd that was bowing to the new Day Child, the same Onizards who had previously refused to help her, thinking she was worthless.

Teltresan? The former non-nature took one look at her new body and gasped. Before she could say anything else, however, a Child of Earth stepped forward and bowed. Her jade skin had become pale with age, but if she had any trouble bowing she did not show it.

Lady Teltresan, please allow me the honor of healing you, she said, her eyes cast to the ground. *I am not worthy of being called Earth's child, but I must make amends for cruelly abandoning an Onizard who needed me.*

Teltresan began to cry. *Mother, I forgive you.*

As the healer did her work, Delbralfi finally let go of Teltresan's tail. Smiling shyly, he said, *I guess I shall see you, then.*

Before the sun sets? Teltresan asked, her tone full of worry.

Of course, my lady, Delbralfi said, shocked that she would even think otherwise. *I shall always be here for you, in sunshine or in starlight.*

Senraeno kept his eyes on the Fire Queen and his claws dangerously close to her throat. He was not going to let her cause any more trouble for the Sandleyr.

Kill me now, child, she said to him privately. *Spare me more dishonor.*

I will not have another death in this Sandleyr, even if it is the death of scum, Senraeno said firmly.

Your Bond's mother screamed in agony before she died of the burns I inflicted. I could have stepped on her and ended her pain, but I let it endure. Surely you could not let the murderer of your Bond's mother go on living when you can end it all now?

You are just giving me more reason why I should not kill you, Senraeno said, after a moment's pause.

What are you talking about, you pathetic fool?

Jena's mother suffered great pains to protect her and raise her to be a kind and caring human. She did not want Jena to become someone who would kill, not even a heartless demon like you. So, out of respect for her memory, I will let you live each day with the knowledge that you killed many who deserved to live happily in this world. I will let you be haunted by the screams of Mekanni and the rage of Delsenni for the rest of your life. That is my justice; I will leave the rest to my mother.

Chapter 36

Deybralfi, after I have carefully reviewed the evidence given to me by the Lady of Day, other trustworthy Onizards, and Zarder Jena, I have decided that I have no choice but to banish you from the Sandleyr. Rulsaesan said as her first act as Leyrque. *You may, however, appeal this decision to the Leyrkan and Lady of Night if you wish,* she added with a smirk.

No, I shall accept this decision, the former Fire Queen said, doing a terrible job of masking her fear of the alternative. *I would not want to live in your Sandleyr anyway,* she added as she flew away. *Good luck ruling the Onizards when you have a human giving you advice and a non-nature as your Lady of Day.*

Zarder and non-Child of Earth are the correct terms, said Teltresan, though she was not paying particular attention to the former Fire Queen now that she posed no threat to the Sandleyr. Where had Delbralfi hidden himself? Why was he suddenly shying away from her? She was worried about what he potentially had to hide from her, and did not dare to hope that perhaps he had feelings for her that he did not want her powers to perceive. What had he said after she was unconscious?

Lady Teltresan, do you have anything to say before I mention my next order of business? Rulsaesan questioned, bringing Teltresan's thoughts back to the business of a ruling Child of Light.

No, Leyrque, I do not, she replied.

Then Watchzard Idenno, come forth!

Idenno showed his head through the Sandleyr entrance. *My lady and Leyrque, what do you ask of me?*

Nothing, Rulsaesan said. *You have given enough of yourself that was unreturned. The only reason you are Watchzard now is that you sacrificed your own future to save mine. I am retiring you from that position, and I hope, my dear friend, that you live the rest of your life in peace.*

Tears filled Idenno's eyes. *Thank you, Leyrque.*

You are welcome, my friend, but if anyone deserves thanks, it is you.

Turning slightly red, the former Watchzard smiled and turned away from the entrance. *I have only done what my heart told me was right. I will wait here for nightfall, to be certain that the demon is truly gone. I am certain the Leyrkan and Lady of Night will be glad to see me.*

I believe they will, Rulsaesan said. *I will send Delbralfi as the official messenger for the Day Kingdom. In the mean time, we must make certain the entire Sandleyr is here for meetings from now on.* She turned to Jena and said, *will you do the honors, Zarder?*

"Of course," Jena said as she turned toward the human leyr. "All humans report! I repeat, all humans report!"

The humans of the Sandleyr walked with looks of complete confusion. Some of them also appeared terrified, while others who saw Jena standing nearby grinned in joyful surprise. Bryn lead the group, completely oblivious to his surroundings. "What under the stars is going on? We heard a great deal of commotion out here earlier, and now we're being called to the Sandleyr meeting as if we were actually important. Where did the second Child of Light come from? Why is Jena standing there?" Realization hit him. "Jena? You are alive? Or am I dreaming?"

She is alive, confirmed Rulsaesan. *She and her Bond Senraeno have saved the Sandleyr with the help of Lady Teltresan. The former Fire Queen has been banished.*

"Jena is alive!" Bryn exclaimed as he rushed toward her and gave her a hug. "It all makes sense now. You have no idea how much I-we all missed you."

"Sorry I tricked you into thinking I was the brightest star in the heavens," Jena said as she laughed. "Bryn, you walked right by the Leyrque without paying her your respect."

Bryn turned to Rulsaesan and bowed. "My apologies, Leyrque. I was distracted by a star falling to the earth."

Rulsaesan's laughter echoed throughout the Sandleyr. *It is forgiven, Bryn. But I am afraid I must halt your reunion with Jena for a moment. There is urgent business we must address.*

"More urgent than Jena being alive? This I must hear."

Bryn of the Sandleyr, Rulsaesan began, *under the former Queen humans were considered inferior because they could not Bond. Due to new evidence, I must discount that ridiculous theory. Therefore, using humans as the Sandleyr's slave labor force will no longer be tolerated. I trust that Zarder Jena and Senraeno will lead the way in bringing equality between our peoples. Perhaps we can even hope for more Zarders in the future.*

That is assuming more Onizards have children in the near future, Leyrque, Teltresan said.

I know. But you never know, we may see new Onizard couples in the near future, Rulsaesan said with a wink only Teltresan saw. *This meeting is dismissed. If you have any questions or concerns, speak to me and I will gladly address them.*

Chapter 37

Delbralfi paced back and forth in his leyr in frustration. He did not dare venture out of his leyr, for chances were great that he would run into Teltresan, and with her new powers she would discover the truth he had declared to the Sandleyr.

It had been wonderful to finally tell her his feelings, and he felt almost free for having said what he had said. But somehow telling her again and telling her alone brought great fear into his heart. He did not know if she had even heard him, and if she had heard him, she could not see him in that way. Why else was she avoiding him? Did she fear what her powers would perceive in him? Or did he dare to hope that she feared her powers would perceive nothing?

It doesn't matter anyway. I'm a son of a traitor, and she's the Lady of Day. I'm not worthy of her. As he continued pacing back and forth, he heard another Onizard outside his leyr. *Teltresan?* he asked hopefully.

You aren't so lucky, I'm afraid, Idenno said as he peeked his head into the leyr. *I just came by to say that I'm proud of you.*

Proud of me? I haven't done anything worthy of anyone being proud of me.

You may think that, but it seems that we have been in a similar predicament, Idenno said. *Hated by the Fire Queen, not knowing if our family is still alive or sane, and being terrified to tell the lady we love the truth. I'm just proud that you were able to admit it in front of the entire Sandleyr. I never even got the guts to admit to my love until it was far too late and she could sense it anyway.*

Delbralfi shrugged. *Well, it didn't do any good. She still doesn't know, and if she does, she doesn't feel the same way about me. She's far too beautiful, and I'm the son of her enemy.*

Have you asked Teltresan how she feels yet? You cannot be certain about that until you do. Besides, you're a handsome Onizard, and you are not the son of her enemy.

Really? Delbralfi asked, skeptical of both points.

I know your true mother, and you look just like her. You can meet her, if you don't believe me; I'm sure Lady Delsenni and Leyrkan Mekanni will be extremely happy to see you.

Delbralfi blinked in confusion. There was something about the way the former Watchzard spoke that told him that Idenno was speaking the truth, and it brought him happiness that he could not explain.

How long have you known this?

I've known you were my nephew since I saw you carrying Deldenno back from the Leyr Grounds, Idenno said.

Delbralfi blinked again. *Why didn't you say anything about it before?*

Would anyone have believed me if I tried?

Delbralfi shrugged. *I suppose not. I doubt that even Teltresan would believe me if I told her that truth.*

You don't have to tell her; she already learned from Jena, and she's happy for you, Idenno said as stepped closer and looked firmly at his nephew. *Listen to me, Delbralfi; I won't bother you about this issue any further, but I will tell you that if you don't tell Teltresan how you feel now, you will regret it for the rest of your life. Take it from me, the King of Love Unreturned.*

As Idenno left, Deldenno returned to the leyr. *Guess what, Bral! Rulsaesan said she needs you to be the messenger to the Night Kingdom. She said Jena will give you more information on why you were chosen.*

Delbralfi smiled. *Well, I cannot refuse my Leyrque. I shall be back in a little while, Delden; I must find my Lady.*

Teltresan stood on the sea wall watching the waves crash against the rocks below. She knew fewer Onizards would bother her if she stood there alone, and she needed time to think about her own problems before she dealt with the pain of others.

Staring at her distorted reflection on the waves, the Child of Light found her thoughts straying to Delbralfi and the pained look he gave her as he let go of her tail and stepped away from the crowd of Onizards surrounding her. No declaration of loyalty could take away the sadness it brought her as she watched him walk away with his head bowed to the ground. Not even her mother's sudden acceptance could diminish the sense of loss she felt from his absence. Her younger self would not have believed it possible that her mother's acceptance would mean relatively nothing to her, but Teltresan's heart only held thoughts for one Onizard. Now she only had to look him in the eyes to tell if he loved her in return, and the implications of that power frightened her.

You've picked a good spot, Rulsaesan said as she landed gracefully on the wall beside Teltresan. Teltresan attempted to bow, but the elder Day Child simply laughed. *We are equals, Teltresan. There is no need for uncomfortable formalities.*

I am sorry, Teltresan said. *I'm still getting used to being respected by the entire Sandleyr.*

Yes, it is certainly difficult to adjust at first, Rulsaesan said as she gave her an almost motherly smile. *I could not understand why I was chosen, and I feared that I would bring about the fall of the Sandleyr all by myself. Then I learned who my friends were, and my dear Deyraeno told me how capable I was. When I looked into his eyes, I became far less worried about the future.*

Teltresan looked at the elder Onizard and smiled. Even without the use of her powers, she could sense Rulsaesan's deep devotion and love for her mate, and she felt saddened that she did not have the courage to speak openly of her love for Delbralfi.

The two of us used to come here often. Deyraeno asked me to be his joinmate here one morning when the sun rose over the water, Rulsaesan said, smiling as she recalled a distant memory. *Of course, Delbralfi would not want to come this close to the water, but I'm sure you two will find a spot to call your own.*

Teltresan hid her eyes in embarrassment. *So you've noticed, then.*

Teltresan, the whole Sandleyr noticed. It was rather hard not to notice, given the situation.

I can't believe I'm really that obvious, Teltresan sighed. *No wonder he was so nervous around me.*

Rulsaesan blinked a few times before she began to laugh hysterically. *Teltresan, you aren't the one who needs to worry about being obvious.*

What do you mean? Teltresan asked curiously, her mental voice full of hope.

I mean you should stop worrying and go speak to him. If you didn't hear what he said, I am terribly sorry for you. Perhaps he will share his memory with you, but it won't be the same.

You've greatly confused me, Rulsaesan, but I will take your advice, Teltresan said as she took off from the wall. *I will let you know if we find our spot.*

Delbralfi waited patiently for Teltresan outside her leyr. He would wait until nightfall if he had to, but he was going to tell her of his feelings again. He had to know for certain if she felt the same way. But each moment he stood outside her leyr carved away at his dwindling hope. He tried to justify things by telling himself that she was probably busy with her new duties, but he did not want to give himself a false hope. Despite what Idenno said, he regretted speaking his feelings to the whole Sandleyr. He feared now that the whole Sandleyr would know of his rejection and his pain.

Teltrena arrived at Delbralfi's leyr, only to be greeted by Deldenno. *He's not here; he went to look for you. I will tell him you came; I'm sure he'll be happy to hear that.*

That won't be necessary, Delden. Could you please tell me where he went?

The Child of Water paused for a moment, as if listening to something only he could hear. Then he grinned and said, *He's waiting for you outside your leyr.*

Without even the courtesy of saying good-bye to Delden, she rushed across the Invitation Hall. A few foolish Onizards tried to stop her to earn her favor, but she quickly scared them away by threatening to reveal their inner secrets to the entire Sandleyr. When she finally arrived, the sight of Delbralfi smiling at her took her breath away. There was something strangely different about him, though she couldn't understand what it was. He looked like the same Onizard she knew and loved, yet there was something greater about him she could not quite see.

Delbralfi, I...um...well, I'm glad to see you.

I'm glad to see you, too, he replied, his voice wavering slightly. *Umm...what do you remember about before you lost consciousness?*

I remember seeing you catch me, and I felt extremely happy to be close to you, even though I thought I was going to die at the time.

Delbralfi smiled. *Did you hear what I said to you?*

You asked me not to leave you. Then I didn't hear anything else.

The Child of Fire laughed nervously. *Well, maybe you should see this, then,* he said as he touched her gently and let her see his memory.

I-I love you. I'm so sorry I never told you before now. I was scared that I'd lose you if I said anything. But Bryn was right; forgive me for being too stupid to tell you that I would miss you if you left this world.

Teltresan stood in blissful shock as she left his memory. *You said that in front of all of the Onizards in the Sandleyr?*

I did, and I meant everything I said, Delbralfi said, grinning in what she knew was an attempt to hide his embarrassment.

Teltresan looked into his eyes and at once felt complete peace, for she could see and feel that he was telling the truth. *Excuse me, Delbralfi. There's something I need to do now.* Turning away from the leyr, she shouted, *All Onizards and humans report! Lady Teltresan has an announcement to make!*

Teltresan, what are you doing? Delbralfi asked, his eyes widening in terror.

The Lady of Day simply smiled and surveyed the growing crowd in front of her. When she was certain everyone who was going to come was there, she said, *It has come to my attention that my beloved friend told me something of extreme importance while I was unconscious. Now that I know he was brave enough to declare his feelings to the entire Sandleyr, I have something to say in return,* Teltresan turned to Delbralfi, smiled, and grasped his tail in her own. *Delbralfi, I love you too. I don't want to start my second life without you by my side.*

Delbralfi grinned as he pulled Teltresan close to him. *I would never even think of leaving your side. It is the most blessed place in the Sandleyr.*

Epilogue, Or Dancing in the Starlight

Mekanni awoke at dusk feeling as if all of his burdens had suddenly been lifted away. For a moment, he thought that he was dead, until he attempted to put weight on his left legs and felt the all-too-normal pain return. Yet even this did not take away from the strange feeling of renewal; it was almost as if some of the strength he had lost many years before had returned to him.

Mek, you must come see this! Senni said, her mental voice filled with joy. Now Mekanni was completely confused, for she had not been truly happy since the night the Fire Queen gained power. But at least he knew part of the reason he felt so invigorated; her happiness and love was the source of what strength he had left.

As he stepped outside of the leyr, he discovered an even stranger sight; Delsenni was standing in the Invitation Hall next to a Child of Fire, and both of them were laughing and crying at the same time.

Leyrkan Mekanni? the strange Onizard asked, his voice filled with nervousness.

I am Mekanni, he answered, though he feared starting the night by speaking to an Onizard that probably either wanted to beg for his favor or harass him based on words spoken by the Fire Queen. Senni's smile told him that this Onizard was not an intruder. What was going on?

I am the messenger of Leyrque Rulsaesan and Lady Teltresan of the Day Kingdom, the glad joinmate of Teltresan. They send hope that their allies in the Kingdom of Night remain strong, and bring the glad news that the Fire Queen is banished forever.

Mekanni was now fully awake, and he smiled with real joy for the first time since Senmani's murder. *So justice has been restored at last. I take it Jena and her Bond Senraeno came to the Sandleyr's aid?*

Yes, and Zarder Jena insisted that I be the messenger, said the Child of Fire, but there was no trace of pride in his statement; in fact, Mekanni sensed what seemed like fear in him.

The Leyrkan of Night sighed. *Please don't be afraid of me; I am a peaceful Onizard. Surely Lady Jena has told you this.*

I am not afraid of you, sir, said the messenger, holding up his tail to illuminate his face and his currently pale lavender eyes. *I am nervous, because Jena told me the other things she learned from you.*

Mekanni took a moment to catch his breath. *Delbralfi.*

The Child of Fire bowed awkwardly and proceeded to tell the rest of his message. *Idenno is no longer a prisoner to the Watchzard duties; he is waiting for you outside. I am a temporary messenger; if you desire it, the evidence of the Fire Queen's crimes against you can stay in the realm of Day and never bother you again.*

No, I would not have that. You are not a bother; you are my son, and I love you as much as I love your mother.

The Night family smiled and joined in a group embracing one another.

Something is still missing, Delsenni said as she pointed up to the Sandleyr entrance with her tail. *You'll have to go drag him down here, Mek. You know how he gets when it's raining outside.*

Mekanni nodded, and after he flew outside he noticed a Child of Water in the distance. With a series of graceful leaps, the Onizard was finishing part of a dance. Very few knew all of its steps, and some of them were in the Day Kingdom permanently. Some of them were not even alive anymore, but the dance still went on, even if it was in shortened form.

The water Onizard turned and froze mid-step, and his face became clear under the starlight. Tears formed in his eyes as he asked, *Mek? Is that really you?*

Mek has returned, Iden, Mekanni said as he slowly and carefully continued the dance.

Inhabitants of the Sandleyr

The Day Kingdom

Deybralfi, the Fire Queen is the ruler of the Day Kingdom until someone inherits her mother's powers and becomes a Child of Light. She bears disdain for her true name, as well as for her subjects. Her curiosity about a human means life for a short time; her anger is deadly.

Lady Rulsaesan has been weakened by the lack of another Child of Light, but some see the birth of her five children as an omen for better things to come.

Deyraeno is the mate of Lady Rulsaesan, and a protective father.

Delbralfi has been called Fire Prince by some and Lord by others, though he privately disowns the Fire Queen and appears to have no ambitions for power. Rather, it is justice and equality he seeks.

Delculble is a son of Rulsaesan and Deyraeno and Bond of Ransenna. The only dramatic thing to happen to this Onizard was his near-drowning at birth.

Deldenno is a son of Rulsaesan and Deyraeno and Bond of Delbralfi. He was named for the Watchzard Idenno, a friend of his parents.

Ransenna is an Onizard who owes her life to Jena after the rescue of her Bond, Delculble. She seems to be a no-nonsense Child of Earth.

Idenno is the Sandleyr's Watchzard, a duty he performs out of honor and loyalty to Rulsaesan. Some might think him morose, but he is a trustworthy Onizard.

Bryn is a human from Jena's former village, Bryn seems to harbor a deep hatred for the Onizards. His bold manner of speaking at times gets him into trouble.

Teltrena is a non-nature, an Onizard forbidden to use her powers because of a past crime. She has tried to avoid controversy for ten years, only to find herself rescued by a handsome Lord and rebelliously healing a hatchling Bonded to a human in the same day.

Ammasan is the deceased ruler of the Day Kingdom. After her mysterious death, no Child of Light took her place, thus allowing the Fire Queen to rule in her stead.

Amsaena and Rulraeno are the daughters of Rulsaesan and Deyraeno. While they have not led as interesting a life as their siblings, they are by no means less loved by their parents.

The Night Kingdom

Leyrkan Mekanni rules the Night Kingdom with his joinmate, Lady Delsenni. Once a powerful Lord, Mekanni has struggled with an illness that frightens many away from his kingdom.

Lady Delsenni rules the Night Kingdom with her joinmate, Leyrkan Mekanni. She takes on the role of protector and nurturer for both her mate and the Zarder.

Jena is a Zarder, at least according to her Bond Senraeno. There has never been a human Bonded to an Onizard, and the Fire Queen would want Jena dead if she knew about her.

Senraeno is a son of Rulsaesan and Deyraeno and the Bond of the human Jena. His naïve nature is tempered with a strong sense of justice.